Da Gama, Cary Grant, and the Election of 1934

Charles Reis Felix

Da Gama, Cary Grant, and the Election of 1934

University of Massachusetts Dartmouth
Center for Portuguese Studies and Culture
North Dartmouth, Massachusetts
2005

PORTUGUESE IN THE AMERICAS 5
General Editor: Frank F. Sousa
Editorial Manager: Gina M. Reis
Copyeditor: Richard Larschan
Graphic Designer: Spencer Ladd
Design Consultant: Memory Holloway
Typesetter: Inês Sena

Da Gama, Cary Grant, and the Election of 1934 / by Charles Reis Felix

This publication was made possible in part by a grant from the Luso-American
Foundation.

For inquiries regarding the Series, please contact:
University of Massachusetts Dartmouth
Center for Portuguese Studies and Culture
285 Old Westport Road
North Dartmouth, MA 02747
Tel. 508-999-8255
Fax: 508-999-9272
Email: greis@umassd.edu
www.portstudies.umassd.edu (publications)

Printed by RPI Printing, Fall River, Massachusetts

Library of Congress Cataloging-in-Publication Data

Felix, Charles Reis.
Da Gama, Cary Grant, and the election of 1934 / Charles Reis Felix.
p. cm. -- (Portuguese in the Americas series)
ISBN: 0-9722561-8-0
1. Portuguese Americans--Fiction. 2. Mayors--Election--Fiction. 3. Massachusetts--
Fiction. 4. Ethnic Groups--Fiction. 5. Depression--Fiction. 6. Boys--Fiction.
I. Title. II. Series.

PS3606.E388D3 2005

For Mona and Matthew

Contents

GEORGE MONTEIRO

The paradox seems to be that the more assiduously an individual works to get away from his beginnings—to leave his early life behind—the more he is fated to live in the past he has tried to leave behind. Thomas Wolfe, it appears, was wrong when he said that you can't go home again. Closer to the truth is that you can't leave your home, no matter how hard you try. James Joyce learned this, writing in Zurich and in Paris, making out of the Dublin life of his youth and early manhood the stories and narrative that have come to epitomize the best of modernist fiction in the English-speaking world.

Charles Reis Felix did not go, technically, into exile as Joyce and so many other writers before him have done, but he did his best to leave New Bedford (his Dublin) behind by, first, going out to Michigan and, then, to California, where he has lived since the late 1940s. Yet, as he was fated to discover, it is his corner of New Bedford in the 1930s—the decade of his youth and adolescence—that *is* his subject.

Charles Reis Felix was born in New Bedford, Massachusetts, in 1923. His parents, José Reis Felix and Ilda Correia Batalha, were immigrants from continental Portugal. He was educated in the public schools of that city, graduating from New Bedford High School in 1941. During 1941-43 he attended the University of Michigan. In 1943 he was drafted into the United States Army, serving for a year in the European theatre. In 1946-47 he was back at the University of Michigan. In 1950 he completed his college education at Stanford University, with a degree in History. Shortly after that, he became an elementary school teacher, retiring in 1984. It is notable that during all those years, and subsequently, he has been writing—fiction and non-fiction. Yet, while of those fictional works *Da Gama, Cary Grant, and the Election of 1934* is the first to be published, its appearance follows on the heels of the publication of *Crossing the Sauer*, a well-received World War II memoir, in 2002, and *Through a Portagee Gate,* an autobiography, in 2004.

Da Gama, Cary Grant, and the Election of 1934 is published as a novel, but, to my mind, it works equally well as a story-cycle. The unifying setting is a place called Gaw—which evokes 'Gee or Portagee. The stories (or chapters, if the reader prefers) add up to a tale of initiation for the central character, the young son of Portuguese immigrants from continental Portugal. As in Ernest Hemingway's stories about Nick Adams in *In Our Time* or Sherwood Anderson's about George Willard in *Winesburg, Ohio,* the boy-hero of Felix's book goes through a series of episodes that serve to shape his understanding of the nature of the world, usually by undeceiving him about the way things really stand or work. Places and sights are worked into Seraphin's travels, first on a walk to the library (which is, potentially, his "pass" out of the world of everything that is Heap Square, an enclave of immigrants and ethnicity) and later on the bus ride enjoyed by virtue of the begged-for bus passes on a Saturday night when the weekly passes run out. And there are set pieces, which, in themselves, shed light on the boy's initiation. The rollicking speechifying of the would-be demagogue, Secundo (*sacana?*) Alves, whose ethnic theme for all seasons and most occasions is the achievement of the Portuguese sailor Vasco da Gama. And the Cary Grant movie, for instance, is lovingly recreated (or synthesized) as a correlative to the way it would have been taken in through the mind and the senses of Seraphin's sister, Laura, a fruit and produce store employee, who allows herself to wallow in the dream world of filmed riches and true love. As in the Anderson and Hemingway story-cycles, the upshot of an episode or incident is not spelled out; there is no wrapping-up, no account of consequences. When the young Azorean immigrant, Anibal, declares his love for Laura during intermission at the movie-house by speaking softly to the back of her head—and this is the first time he has said a word to her—and then moves quickly away without Laura's turning to face him, which she wouldn't think of doing while the lights are on, we know that Laura and this boy are destined to marry (for that is how such choices are made in Portuguese families). But the consequent details are not spelled out. The shape of Laura's future is clear only by implication.

Both comedic and comic, *Da Gama, Cary Grant, and the Election of 1934* gives us a full and generous picture of a time and place that now exist because of words on a page, populated by individualized characters and characteristic incidents. There are the moments of reader recognition, in which things and incidents ring utterly true, for readers who experienced the Great Depression in the larger world they shared with Felix. These range for me from sketches of characters like the chicken butcher and the down-at-the-heels Fred who protects his self-respect and dignity as best he can, to the rendering of the library experience overall, the Sunday night bus trip, and the sister's voluptuous preference for those substantial Old Nick candy bars of our youth. Admirable, too, is the restraint the author shows in presenting the sister's sentimental fate with the boy from the mysterious Azores (feared by many of the Portuguese immigrants from the Continent, as the producer of, perhaps, dangerous boys and men), and the young hero's mildly (if normal) "trickster" relationship with his father—the little game they play over the two turnovers, for example, the way bread in its varieties is used to mark ethnicity, and how the passage of a year in the boy's life just before or at the beginning of puberty lines up incidents in this crucial period of awe and discovery.

"What is fiction in this work and what is autobiography?" Felix was asked. "I don't write fiction," he replied, surprisingly and categorically. "I cannot create make-believe. I am interested in reality." Well, maybe the question was badly put or, perhaps, it was the wrong question. After all, even if "*Da Gama* is 95% non-fiction and 5% fiction," as Felix claims, the world that has emerged from the pages of his book now has a palpable existence in the collective world of the imaginary to be remembered and savored by those who recall Weld Square in the 1930s and those who only now, through this piece of remarkably clear, direct writing, will learn of its existence.

That the fictional work is based on actuality—that is to say, autobiographical experience—does not in any way diminish it as a work of fiction. I am reminded of Hemingway's *Green Hills of Africa*, a work he described as an attempt "to write an absolutely true book to see whether the shape of a country and the pattern of a month's action can, if truly presented, compete with a work of the imagination." The prolific twentieth-century writer Jorge de Sena once characterized his work as entirely autobiographical—memories and other personal material, selected and arranged into narrative sequence when presented as fiction. In that sense—its author's disclaimer notwithstanding—*Da Gama, Cary Grant, and the Election of 1934* is a work of fiction—if that designation really matters—and memorable fiction at that.

AT THE LIBRARY

The chickens were being delivered to the Portagee chicken store, so Seraphin stopped to watch. The farmer stacked the crates on the sidewalk and then left in his junky old truck. The Portagee chicken man was yelling abuse at the plucker, giving him hell about something. He was always yelling at the plucker. I'd sure hate to have to work for that man, Seraphin thought.

The crates were filled with live chickens. This was because the Portuguese liked fresh chickens. They wouldn't buy the dead ones hanging from hooks in the butcher market. "Who knows how long they've been hanging there?" they'd say. So they came to the chicken man, and picked out a live one, and the plucker would take it into the backroom, kill it, pluck the feathers, and bring it out front, show it to the customer, and then wrap it up. Of course, when they were very busy, like on Saturday night, you never saw the plucker. He stayed in the backroom, killing and plucking a mile a minute. Then he wore a rubber apron and big rubber boots, because he used lots of hot water. On Saturday nights this store would be incredibly busy, with all the Portuguese ladies getting a chicken for Sunday dinner. The chicken man's wife and little kid worked here Saturday nights, helping out.

The plucker started taking the crates into the store, one at a time. Inside the store was a big pen made out of chicken wire. It took up about half the store. The plucker would take the crate and release the birds into the pen. That way the chickens would be visible and the customers could pick out the one they wanted.

The birds in the crates on the sidewalk were squawking like crazy. The plucker came out and as he took a crate, he glanced furtively over his shoulder to see if the owner was watching him. He wasn't.

"You know what, kid?" the plucker said to Seraphin.

"What?"

"These chickens shit more than you eat," he said with a harsh laugh.

It was a joke. Seraphin smiled gamely.

The plucker was fourteen years old. His name was Johnny Machado. He didn't know Seraphin, but Seraphin knew him. Ernest Machado, Johnny's younger brother, was in Seraphin's class at school, and that's how he had learned about Johnny. Ernest and Seraphin would both be going into the sixth grade in the fall. Ernest told him that Johnny had been smart in school, but his father wanted him to go to work. So he had quit school and this was the only job he could get.

2

Even before all the crates were taken in, the owner came out with a broom and started sweeping the sidewalk.

A small, white-haired old man came up to him and asked him in Portuguese, "Do you have any eggs today?"

"I have," the owner bellowed. He didn't talk, he bellowed. It was like he thought the old man was across the street. "Fresh ones. Laid this morning."

"How much are they?"

"Fifteen cents a dozen."

"Too much, too much," the old man complained.

"No, not too much. Not for these. These are big eggs. One of these is worth two of the store's."

He leaned on the broom and waited for the old man to decide.

"And how is your son, *Senhor* Tavares?" the chicken man asked. "Still sick?"

"Yes. Yes. He can't eat. Can't keep his food down."

"The doctor helps?"

"No. The doctor doesn't know what it is. My son knows what it is. It's the chemicals they use to make the rayon. They make him sick."

"The doctors are only good to say, 'Give me the two dollars, and come back next week,'" the chicken man said.

"The doctor tells him to quit that job. But how is he going to quit that job? He has a wife and three children to feed. He can't quit that job. How can he quit that job? Tell me—how can he quit that job?" Then the old man said a whole sentence in English—"Advices are easy to give."

"The doctors kill as many as they cure," the chicken man said. "In my land they tell this story. A farmer had three sons. The first son liked to beg. The second son liked to steal. And the third son liked to kill. 'What shall I do with my sons?' the farmer thought. Then he said, 'I know what I'll do. The one who likes to beg, I shall make him into a priest. The one who likes to steal, I shall make him into a lawyer. And the one who likes to kill, I shall make him into a doctor.'"

"Let me look at the eggs," the old man said dolefully.

They went inside the store.

Just as Seraphin was about to go, a big mob of people started coming by. They were mostly girls and women, with just a few fellows. These were the workers from the shirt sweatshop, which was in the old Mayhew Mill, two blocks past Heap Square. It was early in the afternoon, just a little after one, but this was the summertime, and in the summertime the shirt shop let out early on Wednesday afternoons. But then the workers had to make that time up Saturday morning.

One of the workers at the shirt shop was a French youth, a boy they called Sing Sing. Everybody said he was a crook. Sing Sing was pale, slight of build. He came by walking with a pretty French girl about his own age. He was laughing and talking animatedly to her and she was laughing back. Next door to the Portagee chicken man was the Polish bar, and suddenly the screen door of the Polish bar flew open and a heavy, red-faced man came hurtling out. "You somnabitch!" he yelled at Sing Sing. He waved a clenched fist in the air. "Ahm gonna fix you!" He bobbed his head emphatically in promise.

Sing Sing and the girl had turned at the first shout. The girl was thunderstruck and Sing Sing flushed, but he turned his eyes from the man with a very careful, impassive expression. He and the girl kept walking, and the man went back into the bar.

That was the thing about Heap Square, Seraphin thought. You never knew what was going to happen. He had even seen a man arrested here once. The man was drunk and wouldn't leave the Greek's ice cream and candy store. He kept staggering from one little white table to another, all the while making a speech. The only thing was, he was so drunk you couldn't understand what he was saying. The Greek, who was a very crabby man, telephoned the police station, which was just a few doors away. A policeman came immediately. He was a man

3

of enormous height and girth. He must have weighed three hundred pounds. His blue uniform draped over him like a tent. He was enraged when he saw the drunk. "I thought I told you to go home!" he shouted at the drunk. He twisted the drunk's arms behind him and put on the cuffs. The drunk offered no resistance and apologetically tried to explain. "Don't talk to me!" the policeman shouted. "Who do you think you are?" He grabbed the drunk by the upper arm and jerked him out of the store. And off they went to the police station, the policeman jerking the drunk along, the drunk still trying to explain, and the policeman yelling, "Shut up!" and Seraphin following the two of them, trailing a close but wary distance behind.

The chickens were now inside the chicken store and there was nothing else happening, so Seraphin went on. Next to the chicken store was the Polish bar, and then the Jewish shoestore, Kriegelbaum's. In the window—heavy, men's working shoes. Then came the Globe Theatre.

There were scenes from the various movies on the wall. They were behind glass. There were two separate displays, *Now Playing* and *Coming Attractions*. Under the *Now Playing* sign was a lousy picture with Kay Francis. Every scene from the Kay Francis picture was the same pose—a sad-looking Kay Francis standing there in her living room, talking to some dumb-looking guy with a thin mustache and wearing a suit and tie. There was no action.

Kay Francis was *Wednesday and Thursday*, but what Seraphin was really interested in was *Coming Attractions, Friday and Saturday.* That's when the Globe showed the best pictures. Seraphin stepped sideways to the *Coming Attractions* display.

Darn. It was a North Pole picture with Richard Arlen. There was Richard Arlen swaddled in furs, just his face showing, with the familiar Richard Arlen look—a worried expression and puffed-out cheeks. Seraphin didn't like North Pole pictures, because there was too much snow. It was too monotonous; the action took place in one of only two places—either out in the white and unending expanse of snow or inside a snug cabin.

That was *Trail of the Yukon.* The picture with it looked much better. It featured Seraphin's favorite cowboy, Tom Tyler. Tom Tyler looked like a cowboy should look, tall, handsome, lean, not old and fat like Jack Hoxie or Hoot Gibson. Seraphin studied each Tom Tyler scene carefully.

4

And there was also the accompanying chapter picture, with Ralph Graves. Chapter Six was this week. Seraphin had only seen Chapter One of this serial. It ended with a trap door suddenly opening and Ralph Graves falling into a pit. Then with Ralph Graves trapped down at the bottom of the pit, the bad guys threw a switch, and this strange-looking machinery started up, a huge wheel started turning, and this wheel began to sink down into the pit, slowly turning round and round, and at the bottom of the pit was Ralph Graves, waiting, flat on his back, looking up at the descending wheel getting ever closer and closer, and there was no way he could slip by it, because the sides of the wheel just about touched the sides of the pit, and it was almost up to him, it was pressing against his stomach and it was going to crush him and there was no escape, and then the chapter picture ended and the screen said: *To be continued.* Seraphin had asked a hundred guys if they had seen Chapter Two. He wanted to find out how Ralph Graves got out of it, but he never found anybody who had seen Chapter Two. It was driving him crazy.

Seraphin knew he wouldn't be going to the Globe this Saturday afternoon. He didn't have any money. That was why he was glad it was a North Pole picture, because then he wouldn't feel so bad about missing it. But he sure would like to see Tom Tyler and the chapter picture.

Next to the Globe was the library. This was his destination. The library was on the corner where Heap Square ended, or began, depending on how you looked at it.

The library building had two stories. It was made of brick but the roof was wood. In one corner of the roof there was a great big turret. He always looked at the turret. He liked looking at it. It reminded him of a castle. The monotonous-looking, three-tenement houses in the North End were square and box-like. There wasn't a single turret in the bunch.

There was a small insert of frosted glass in the heavy wooden door. On the glass was painted:

North End Branch
Gaw Free Public Library

Seraphin took the door by the knob, opened it, and stepped inside.

The police station was downstairs. The entrance to the police station was at the other end of the building. The library was upstairs. The wide, winding staircase was before him. But just a few feet from him, to his left, was a door. Behind that door was the police. It was a back door and he had never seen it used. But still—behind that door was the police.

Keeping his eye on the door, he started up the stairs. He stepped as lightly as he could. He did not want to alert the police that he was here. And just then, as if they knew he was here, he heard the great deep-throated bull laughter coming from behind that door, and he felt the walls and the stairs under him shaking from heavy, ponderous foot-steps. Somebody was coming close to that door! And Seraphin felt his heart beating wildly. How many times had he imagined it—the enor-mous three-hundred-pound cop springing out from behind the door and grabbing him and dragging him into the police station and throw-ing him into a cell and accusing him? Accusing him of what? He did-n't know and it didn't matter. For his situation would be hopeless. For how could he prove his innocence? It would be his word against theirs, and who would believe him? Being innocent didn't help. He had found that out from Kriegelbaum's kid. One afternoon he had been walking through Heap Square, and this kid suddenly darted out from Kriegelbaum's store and started screaming at the top of his lungs and pointing at him. "Dad! Dad! Come here! I found the boy who did it! Come quick! I found him!" People were stopping and staring at Seraphin. They looked at him like he was guilty. Seraphin stood there, mute and shocked. The kid, about his own age, was blocking his way. Seraphin had never seen this kid before in his life. Later on he found out it was Kriegelbaum's kid. And then Kriegelbaum came running out of the store. Seraphin knew it was serious from the wild expression on Kriegelbaum's face and the way he ran out. Kriegelbaum was an old guy with a potbelly, and normally he moved only with a slow dignity, but here he was sprinting. "He's the one, Dad! He's the one who did it!" the kid was screaming. And Seraphin got the sudden feeling that it was something dirty he was supposed to have done, something to do with sex organs. What else could have excited the Kriegelbaums so much? And then Kriegelbaum looked carefully at Seraphin and recognized him and his face changed. "That's the cobbler's son," Kriegelbaum said disgustedly to his kid. "It's all right," he said to Seraphin and smiled apologetically. "He made a mistake." He put his arm around his kid's shoulders and took him back into the shoestore. Seraphin was left on the sidewalk, alone and shaken. It had all happened so fast, and now he was free. The moment was over. But the memory was just beginning. The fear, the panic, that stayed with you. Mr. Kriegelbaum knew him and knew that he didn't do bad things. But suppose it hadn't been Mr. Kriegelbaum. Suppose it had been a man who didn't know him. What then? The kid was so positive. Anybody would have believed him. That's why Seraphin was so afraid of being accused.

The back door to the police station did not open, and Seraphin made it safely to the top of the stairs. There were two swinging doors before him that opened into the library. He pushed on the right-hand one and he was in the library.

To his right was the newspaper room. He went by it and looked in. It didn't have a door; one side of the room was open. The newspaper room consisted of a large rectangular table with wooden chairs at all four sides of the table. The rack holding the newspapers was in the back of the room by the window. Above the rack and a little to the left, on the wall, was an ominous injunction in thick black block-letters: NO LOITERING. That sign always kind of scared Seraphin. He always felt he was loitering and would be kicked out.

Of course, that was a very common sign in Gaw. It was like there was a war going on in Gaw against loiterers. Everywhere you went, you saw that sign. Take along the Avenue where all the stores were. The buildings along the Avenue were all pretty much the same, made out of wood, with the store on the street level and two tenements above the store. Alongside the store would be a door, and then behind the door were narrow stairs leading to the two tenements above. But the landlord did not want anyone hanging around the bottom of the stairs, so above almost every doorway there was posted a POSITIVELY NO LOITERING sign.

That sign was in the newspaper room as a warning to the old men. In the summertime this room was deserted, but in the wintertime the old men flocked here. It was a way to keep warm. The old men lived alone and they were fleeing their unheated tenements. In the tenement houses of Gaw there wasn't one big boiler that provided the heat for the whole house. Each tenement had its own stove and provided its own heat, and if you didn't have any money to buy coal, then your tenement would be cold.

So the men came here. The colder it got, the more old men there would be who suddenly got interested in newspapers. When it was

7

freezing outside, every chair around the table would be taken and would stay occupied till closing time. Two or three of the old men would actually be reading a newspaper. The rest would be half-dozing, nodding in the pleasant heat, with an open newspaper before them. The steam radiator under the window would be hissing, fizzing, crackling, and exploding. That would be the only sound. The old men did not talk to one another. That was against the library rules and they did not want to jeopardize their stay here. But, actually, they did not look like they wanted to talk to each other. They seemed content to just sit back and soak in the enervating heat.

They were loitering. Seraphin knew they were. And Seraphin knew the librarian knew they were loitering. But the librarian never once came over and kicked them out. She had a heart, that was the reason.

Seraphin looked in the newspaper room. There was only one person in there. Seraphin knew him. It was Fred Farnsworth, whom everybody called just Fred. Fred lived alone in an attic tenement on Seraphin's street. He had never married. He was old, in his sixties, with white hair. He was tall and thin. There wasn't an ounce of fat on him, because he didn't eat much and he walked a lot. He told Seraphin once that when he was younger he used to walk from Gaw to Shefford and back on Sundays. That was a total distance of thirty miles. Of course, he didn't go on walks like that now, but he still liked to walk. You'd see him all over the North End, walking. He spent a lot of time in the library reading newspapers, too. He could do that, walking and reading, because he didn't work. He hadn't worked for a few years. Fred was from England and he had been a weaver in the Gaw cotton mills for many, many years. Weaving is the most highly-skilled job in the mill, but when the mills started closing down, Fred was laid off and he was never able to find another job again.

After reading the newspapers, Fred often went across the street to Pa's shop. Pa was very much interested in the news, and Fred had a good memory, so he would tell Pa about the news articles he had just read. Pa and Fred had their own way of doing things. Pa wouldn't stop his work. He'd keep working on the shoe, standing by his workbench, facing the street. Fred would stand by him, telling him the news. Then at frequent intervals, Fred would pause and Pa would repeat back to him what Fred had just said, in summarized form. That was Pa's way of checking to see if he had understood the story correctly. "That's right, that's what Roosevelt wants to do," or, "That's right, he buried her in her own garden," Fred would say in verification, and then he'd continue.

But Fred was very uneasy about hanging around the shop. He knew that Pa wasn't making any money off him. And hangers-on can give a business a bad name. So if a paying customer came in the shop, Fred would stop in midsentence, bid a hasty good-bye, and bolt out the door. He didn't want to impose himself on anyone. That's how he was. If you met him on the street, he waited for you to recognize him first. If you didn't speak to him first, he would go right by you, head straight, his face blank. He would understand that you didn't want to talk to him at that given time and place. But if you said, "Hello, Fred," his face would break out into a big smile, and he would be eager to talk to you.

That was why when Seraphin now looked into the newspaper room, Fred, who was always very alert, looked up from his newspaper and looked directly at Seraphin, but gave him no sign of recognition. Seraphin understood. It was Fred's way. This was not the place to acknowledge acquaintanceship. The librarian was looking at them. It was safer not to say anything. So Seraphin looked at Fred as if he were a stranger and walked on by. And Seraphin said to himself, "What a great spy I would make." He had learned from numerous spy pictures that the cardinal rule a spy must follow is not to show any recognition of people he knows in public places but to wait till they were alone in a safe place.

The librarian sat at her desk at the far end of the library. Seraphin walked toward her. There was only open space going down the middle of the library. To his right were the book stacks. To his left were long tables and chairs, put there for people who might want to sit and read.

When Seraphin got just about to the center of the library, he turned toward the magazine rack, which was against the wall on his left. He took the *American Boy* magazine and sat at one of the long tables, his back to the wall. Whenever he could, he sat with his back to the wall. He didn't like the idea of people being able to sneak up on him from behind and catch him by surprise.

The librarian and Fred were the only two people in the library, beside himself. He was sitting exactly halfway between the librarian and Fred. He didn't want to feel too close to either one, especially to the librarian. This way he could see her but she was a safe distance away.

9

And he could see Fred and Fred was a safe distance away, too. Neither one of them could sneak up on him. And neither one was close enough to cough or rustle papers or otherwise interfere with his reading. He didn't like people close to him when he read. They didn't have to make a lot of noise. Just their shifting and squirming in their seats bothered him. Even if they just picked their nose, it bothered him.

She was a good librarian. She had always been the librarian here, ever since he could remember. He liked her. She scared him, but he liked her. She kept the library quiet, the way it was supposed to be. She was a small, gray-haired woman, spare as a bird, with a hawk-like nose. She was silent. She never spoke. She never smiled. She rarely left her desk. But she controlled the library. She had these burning eyes. Let two or three kids come in and start whispering and she would take a ruler and slap it down decisively against the top of her desk, twice, in quick succession, the sound ringing out sharply like two pistol shots, and everybody in the library would jump, and the two kids would look at her, and her burning eyes would hold them, and they would slink off.

And she was alert. She knew everything that was going on in her library. Even now. She wasn't looking at him. But he knew she was aware of him. He could feel her presence. She sent out rays. She was glad he was here. She was lonesome for company, he could feel it. And she knew he behaved himself.

Seraphin opened the oversized, dark-green, stiff-board covers on the outside of the *American Boy*. The *American Boy* cover stared up at him—bright and fresh and crisp and clean! The new *American Boy* had come in! Probably he was the first person to touch it! The new *American Boy*! What a piece of luck! He had come here, and come here, and come here, waiting for this new issue, and just about when he had gotten to the point of believing it would never come, it had come!

And this issue had an article on Babe Ruth! Beside the exciting three or four stories it always had! Wow! But he had his own way of reading the magazine. He could plunge in and read the best things first and read everything fast and then it would soon be over. But he made himself read slowly and he studied all the drawings and photographs. But more than that, he tried to keep from reading the best things for as long as he could stand it. He tried to save them for another day. After all, if he read this magazine in one day, then there would be nothing to read for a whole month. It was better to stall around, make it last. He knew how to procrastinate, delay the pleasure. So he did not turn to the Babe Ruth article. Instead he began studying the ads in the front of the magazine. He read every word describing the product. He lost himself in all those treasures, the perfect heavy jackknife with all those different blades, the streamlined red bicycle, and the beautiful Buster Brown shoes. The Buster Brown shoes brought an especially sharp pang of sadness and loss to Seraphin, for there was a Buster Brown Club he could join if only he could buy a pair of Buster Brown shoes. The Buster Brown Club put out a magazine and they sent this magazine to every club member free of charge. The magazine was filled with stories, mysteries, puzzles, and exciting things like that. But the catch was you couldn't join the club till you bought a pair of Buster Brown shoes. The shoestore owner gave you a piece of paper and you sent that paper in. But the shoestore owner wouldn't give you that paper till you bought the shoes. Seraphin had looked at all the shoestore windows in the North End. None of the shoestores carried Buster Brown shoes. And he knew why—they were expensive. He could tell that from the ad; the picture showed a pair of shoes and they were really well made. So even if there was a Buster Brown shoestore in the North End, Ma wouldn't buy them, because they were too expensive. So he was stuck. He could not join the Buster Brown Club. He could not get the Buster Brown Club magazine. But, boy, what he wouldn't give to be a member.

Seraphin then thought of something else he could do. He could go over to the stacks, to the kids' book section. It would be a waste of time because he had read every book they had, but he hadn't been over there for quite a while, so he decided he would do it.

They didn't have very many books for kids, just three shelves. He stood before them. Same old stuff. *Tom Sawyer, Call of the Wild*—that was a great book. *White Fang. Grimm's Fairy Tales.* He liked fairy tales. He liked the magic in them. *Story of a Bad Boy* by Thomas Bailey Aldrich. That was a good book. Two books by Ralph Henry Barbour and one by William Heyliger—they were two good writers; they wrote sport stories. *Penrod* by Booth Tarkington. Then he saw *Lorna Doone* and sighed. That was the one book in the kids' section he had never read. *Lorna Doone* was a heavy, grim-looking book. It weighed a ton. Its covers were black, put on by the library. They were about half an

11

inch thick. Those thick black covers oppressed the spirit, and whenever he saw the book on the shelf he had a feeling of impending doom. He had tried to read it. Many times when he was desperate for something to read, he had picked it up, read a paragraph here and there, tried to get into it, but somehow he never could. He always put *Lorna Doone* back on the shelf. And look at the dust on the covers. Nobody was taking it out. He guessed everybody felt the same way he did about it.

Then Seraphin noticed a book with an unfamiliar color. Light blue. Holding his breath in disbelief he reached for the book. The library had not rebound the book. The front cover was the original cover; it showed a painting of a midshipman in his whites and a vessel sailing away in the distance. He read the title: *An Annapolis Plebe.* And the author, whose name was below the midshipman's feet: *Lieut. Commander Edward L. Beach U.S.N.* He quickly turned some pages. It was great. Lots of conversation. That meant it was a good book. And then to cinch it, he came across an illustration. It was a full page on glossy paper. It was a painting, but no bright colors, just white, gray, and black. And the painting was carefully done, with lots of detail, the kind of illustration he liked. It showed a midshipman standing at attention with his cap in his hand. Facing him was this officer, middle-aged, grave, stern. The officer was seated at a table and he held a piece of paper in his hand. Obviously, from the officer's expression, the midshipman was in big trouble. And on the bottom of the illustration was the caption: *"I am not guilty," said Robert.* Seraphin just *knew* this was going to be a good book! He turned to the last page of the book. It had 435 pages. Good, the longer the better.

But where had this book come from? It had never been here before—he would have seen it one of those hundred times he had been here. And he knew the library hadn't just bought it. Far from being new, it showed every sign of use and age. He turned to the back, where there was a white form glued to the inside back cover. It had little slots where the librarian stamped the due date every time the book went out. The white form was crisp and clean. There wasn't a single due date on it. This book had never been taken out of the library.

He opened the book. A beautiful gold seal was glued to the inside of the front cover. On the seal were two pillars standing straight up like in a Greek building. Some lions were at the base of the pillars, kind of leaning on them with their front paws. At the top of the seal were embossed the words: *Ex Libris.* And between the two pillars someone had written in pen with beautiful handwriting: *Oliver Mayhew III.*

The Mayhew Mill. Ma said that Oliver Mayhew had died, the grandfather who originally started the mill. It was started in 1883; Seraphin had seen the year carved out of stone over the entrance to the mill. In the old days when Ma first came from Portugal, Oliver Mayhew had been the mayor of Gaw. But then he died and some years later his son, Oliver Mayhew II, became the mayor and he was still the mayor today. This Mayor Mayhew also had a son, Oliver Mayhew III, and it was this Oliver Mayhew III who had owned this book. Seraphin had seen a picture of Mayor Mayhew and his son in a recent Sunday edition of the *Evening Herald.* The son looked like he was in his late thirties. What was he doing with *An Annapolis Plebe,* which was obviously a kid's book? Seraphin was puzzled by this question. Then he turned a couple of pages and found the answer. *An Annapolis Plebe* was copyrighted in 1907—when Oliver Mayhew III would have been about *ten years old!* This book had been given to Oliver Mayhew III as a Christmas or birthday present when he was ten years old, and the other day he had been looking his books over and he realized he had outgrown this book, so he decided to give it to the library. That was it.

Seraphin closed the book and stared dreamily at the front cover— at the midshipman in his whites standing with his bayoneted rifle. This book, this very book in his hands, had been owned by a rich boy, and now he was going to read the very same book, turn the very same pages the rich boy had turned. The rich boy had been absorbed by this book, held by it, and now he would be, too. He felt close to the rich boy. He felt that, in some strange way, they were equals. He felt that he and Oliver Mayhew III were friends—when Oliver was young. And he felt grateful to the Mayhew family for giving this book to the library. They could have kept it or they could have just thrown it away. And then he would never have had a chance to read it. It was very thoughtful of them to give it to the library. He was glad Mayor Mayhew was mayor of Gaw. If he was old enough to vote, that's who he'd vote for—Mayor Mayhew. He had a nice family, a son who was a good, generous man.

Seraphin left the stacks but with him went *An Annapolis Plebe.* He returned to his old seat. He pushed the *American Boy* aside. He was going to read just one chapter of *An Annapolis Plebe* and no more. He wanted to test the book out, to see if he was right, that it was a darn good book.

Chapter I was called "A Competitive Examination." He read it his slow, lingering way, often reading paragraphs twice. He wanted to implant everything in his head. He didn't want to miss a single line, and he also wanted to make the reading last as long as possible.

Robert Drake, a poor boy but honest, was taking the entrance exam to the Naval Academy. It took three days and Principal Harris of Garfield High was giving it. Thirty young men were taking it. On the first day Robert noticed a rich boy, James Hillman, cheating on the exam. So Robert waited in the coat room after passing in his papers, and when Hillman came in he said to him:

14

> "You have been up to your old tricks again, Jim Hillman! You cheated all through the examination! You had books under your coat and used them all along! I saw you!"
>
> "That's not true!" cried out young Hillman. "You can't prove it!"
>
> Immediately upon this the first speaker jumped forward and tore open Hillman's coat out of which dropped two books.
>
> Hillman stood aghast.
>
> "Not true, you say," exclaimed the young man who had accosted Hillman. "Here is a grammar, and a United States History, and the name 'James D. Hillman' on the fly leaf of each. Take them, you shameful cheat!" And with this the speaker threw the books at Hillman's head.
>
> "You would make a nice midshipman, wouldn't you!" he continued wrathfully. "Now if you come to this examination tomorrow I shall denounce you to Mr. Harris. A fellow who would try to win an examination by cheating is not the kind to go to Annapolis."
>
> "I'll get even with you for this, Bob Drake!" cried out the other, who by this time had recovered a little of his composure. "This is a put up job; those books never fell out of my coat; you fixed it up yourself. You are afraid I am going to win this appointment and think you can scare me out! Who are you to call me a cheat? My father is a railroad owner and yours is nothing but his clerk!"
>
> "My father may be but a clerk, but he is an honest man and I am proud of him; your father may be rich but I know you to be a cheat."
>
> The words uttered with great contempt took away Hillman's power

of denial. He picked up his books and left the building, muttering, "I'll fix you for this, Bob Drake."

That night Robert told his father that he intended to denounce James Hillman to Principal Harris the next day.

"My son," said Mr. Drake, "remember that Mr. Hillman is my employer, a just and generous one. Should you expose and disgrace his son as you have said you will, I cannot conceive that he would retain me in his employ, and where could I get another position, and how provide those things, now above all times, so necessary for your mother? You tell me there are no other witnesses. Now if you should denounce James Hillman, and he should deny your charge, how could you prove it? Think of everything, Robert. I will not coerce you, but shall leave you to act as your own conscience and judgment dictate."

It was not long before Robert decided that he would have to keep quiet about James Hillman; but in his own mind he bitterly resented the roguery of that young aspirant for naval honors.

15

So Robert was on the spot. He didn't dare denounce James Hillman but he was risking losing the Academy appointment to a cheater. It wasn't fair, but what was he to do?

Seraphin looked up from the book and tried to suppress a radiant smile. The book was perfect. He closed *An Annapolis Plebe* and just sat there, not reading, just daydreaming. A feeling of great happiness descended upon him. It wasn't just the excitement of finding a new book nor the pleasure of anticipation of 400 more pages of Robert Drake's further adventures. There was something about the library that always filled him with contentment. It was like being in a church. So peaceful and quiet. All the noise and striving and contention of Heap Square seemed far away. You could sit here and think and no one would bother you.

He liked the smell of the library. Every place had its own smell. On Saturday afternoons the Globe Theatre smelled of disinfectant and buttered popcorn and stale cigarette smoke left over from the night before. The Old Colony Fruit Store smelled of rotting fruit. Pa's shop had its own smell of fresh leather sheets, new rubber heels, shoe polish, hot wax that he used in the stitcher, old shoes with individual peculiarities of human foot-odors, rusty old nails and worn-out soles on the floor, and dust and dirt everywhere. Now the smell of the library was different. It was a faint smell but pervasive. The moment you opened the library doors you inhaled it. It was not an unpleasant smell, certainly not musty, and yet it was a strange smell. He could not decipher it like he could the mixture in Pa's shop. Was the basic ingredient the smell of undisturbed books? Heavy library covers, black ink, dry pages, glued bindings, mixed in with old wood floors and massive oak tables, the faint smell of age and learning. Seraphin inhaled deeply through his nose. Yes, it was there. Just enough to tell. The mystery of the library smell.

The natural light in the library was restful. Because there weren't too many windows, the light was never glaring, but always rather shadowy, almost gloomy. He liked that. And in the summertime the shadows were cool. Coming off the hot street into the library was like finding an oasis with lots of trees out on the desert.

Behind him on the wall was a large clock. Its pendulum swung back and forth. Tick-tock. Tick-tock. Tick-tock. That was the only sound in the library.

The clock ticking. The cool shadows. The smell he loved. The library was as it always had been and always would be, all the details correct and proper. Everything was as it should be. Everything was in its place. The gray-haired, silent librarian was seated behind her desk, where she was supposed to be. Old Fred Farnsworth was in the newspaper room, where he was supposed to be. And he was at the long table in the middle of the library, where he was supposed to be. Everybody was where they were supposed to be. It was like something perfect and fixed in time and space. Everything was as it should be.

But now it was time for action. He took *An Annapolis Plebe* back to the stacks and hid it behind *Lorna Doone.* No one would think to look for it there. He wanted to take *An Annapolis Plebe* home to read but he had not brought his library card. Why should he have? Who would have guessed there would be a book to take out? Tomorrow afternoon he would return with his library card and claim his treasure. For just a moment, he worried. Could someone go poking around the shelves and beat him to it? Suppose he came tomorrow and *An Annapolis Plebe* was gone? He just would have to keep his fingers crossed and take that chance.

He returned to the *American Boy.* Everything was great. He had lots to read. And by the time he took *An Annapolis Plebe* home and dawdled over it for as long as he could, and came back and finished the *American Boy*, why, by that time the new issue of his second favorite magazine, *Boys' Life*, should be in. And by the time he finished *Boys' Life*, the new issue of his third favorite magazine, *Open Road for Boys*, should be in. Every month he read all three of those magazines from cover to cover.

After a few more minutes Seraphin got up and left the library. Once outside he crossed the street and went over to his father's shop, which was also in Heap Square. He wasn't too surprised when he walked up the steps to see Fred Farnsworth there talking to Pa. Pa left the door open in the summertime to try and get a little breeze in the shop, so Seraphin just walked in and slipped by Fred and went over to the only chair in the place and sat down and waited for Fred to finish.

17

Fred was standing by Pa, and Pa had a knife in his hand and was trimming the edges of a new leather sole he had sewed on a shoe. That was just a rough trim. Later he would take that shoe and turn on his big machine at the back of the shop and sand the sole down on a whirring wheel till it was perfect.

"What a city that must be," Pa said, laughing. "They must have more crooks in City Hall than they have in the jails!"

"It would seem so," Fred said mildly.

"We are lucky here in the city of Gaw," Pa said. "We have never had an Irish mayor."

"And you know what they found out about the Mayor's daughter?" Fred continued. "She's been living in Florida all these years, but the Mayor has her listed as his office assistant. She gets a high salary, three thousand dollars a year. Every two weeks the City sends her a check in Florida. All the checks come back canceled on a Florida bank."

Pa's mouth fell open. "She lives in Florida and the City sends her the check for work she does not do?"

"Yes," Fred said, smiling.

Pa shook his head in disbelief. "Crooks. Even the women are crooks. What a race."

"And they found that the Mayor's brother-in-law had two trucks and he leased them to the City. That was all right, but I guess he wanted to make a little extra money, because he charged the City for *seven* trucks! Seven trucks, Joe!"

"He owned two trucks and charged the City for seven?"

"Yes."

"The Irish. . . ," Pa began, and burst into raucous laughter. He tried again. "The Irish. . . ," and he started to laugh uncontrollably. He began making little noises deep inside him.

"When the State Police went to the brother-in-law's house, they searched his house," Fred said, "and in the garage they found a shoe box underneath some old rags. There was fifty thousand dollars cash in the shoe box. And they asked the brother-in-law about the money, where it came from, and he said, 'I don't know how it got there.'"

This was too much for Pa. He was convulsed with laughter. "He didn't know how. . . ," he gasped. Pa fell upon his workbench in weakness. "He didn't. . . ," he wheezed. Tears popped out of his eyes and started running down his cheeks. He gave a sudden shriek of a laugh, then for an instant his laughter became soundless, only the grimace on his face showing the fit was still upon him, and then he was wheezing, and then he was groaning, as if in pain.

Fred and Seraphin were both laughing, too, so infectious was Pa's enjoyment.

"Ooooohh," Pa said, straightening up and trying to get control of himself.

"It's a terrible scandal," Fred said. "It makes Massachusetts look like we don't know how to govern ourselves."

"Fred, I will tell you one thing," Pa said. "The Irish are smart. They don't take a gun and rob a bank. They rob in smart ways. And they go to jail for a short sentence. And then they come out and run for office again, and the people elect them again," and he started to laugh again, although more moderately.

"The judge put only five hundred dollars bail on the son," Fred said. "The son misappropriated over two hundred thousand dollars."

"You know why, Fred? You know why? Because the judge is Irish, too. They're all in this thing to steal together, like gypsies! Fred, I tell you, the gypsies come in my shop, and while the mother is talking to me, the little girl is in the back grabbing a box of nails—it's true! They work together. The Irish are like that. Each knows what the other is taking and then they all share in it later. It's a family of thieves."

Just then Jimmy started up the steps to the shop. Jimmy was a big

man and he had an enormous beer belly. He spent his time in the barroom when he wasn't going around, picking up numbers.

Jimmy came up the three steps slowly, hoisting himself up one step
at a time. He was red-faced and out-of-breath.

Fred quickly stepped aside and Jimmy panted, "What have you got
for me, Joe?"

"You're late, Jimmy! I didn't think you were coming today," Pa said.

"Yeah, I am late," Jimmy admitted. "I got held up, Joe."

Pa reached down into the little metal cash box he kept on the floor
behind the counter. He brought up a penny and laid it on the counter.

"I'm going to play the address of my shop, Jimmy. Eight-six-eight.
I got a hunch on this number."

19

If today's number came out eight-six-eight, Pa would win five dollars for his penny.

Jimmy took the penny and wrote down Pa's number in a tiny notebook with the stub of a pencil.

"Okay, Joe. I'll see you tomorrow."

Jimmy turned to go. Fred, who was still in the shop, did not play
the numbers because he had no money.

Pa looked after Jimmy in a panic of indecision.

Jimmy went out the door and was on the top step.

"Jimmy," Pa cried. "Come back!"

Jimmy came back in.

"By God, Jimmy, I feel lucky today!" Pa exclaimed, shaking his fist
in the air. "Give me back that penny!"

Jimmy gave him back the penny. Pa reached down in his cash box
and came up with a nickel. "Five cents on eight-six-eight straight,
Jimmy. I got a big hunch on this number!"

Jimmy took the nickel and added something by Pa's name in his
notebook.

If eight-six-eight came out, Pa would now win twenty-five dollars.

"Okay, Joe. See you tomorrow," Jimmy said again and went out.

"Maybe I win today," Pa said musingly. "It's about time that I win."

Jimmy started walking down the sidewalk in front of Pa's window.
Pa looked after him thoughtfully. "He's too fat, Fred. Someday he's
going to drop dead in the street."

Pa would not see Jimmy again today. Jimmy did not come around to say what the winning number was. In the late afternoon Harry the Englishman who ran a little fish and chips restaurant across the street usually stopped by and told Pa the number that had come out that day, but if he didn't, Pa just stepped to the doorway and hailed one of his passing customers. They always knew. A lot of people around Heap Square played the numbers.

After a while, Fred left and it was then that Pa turned to Seraphin.

"You wanna go to the Carbarn and get some change for me, Seraphin? I'm all out of change."

"Sure, Pa."

Pa went to the rear of the shop and turned his back to the window, so he could not be seen. He pulled a big roll of bills out of his pocket, took the rubber band off it, and peeled off a five. He gave the five to Seraphin.

"Tell him it's for Joe the Cobbler."

"Okay, Pa."

Seraphin folded the bill twice and wrapped his fist around it and stuck the fist and the enclosed bill deep into his pocket. He would keep them both in his pocket till he got to the Carbarn. That way he'd know where that five dollars was every second of the way.

So Seraphin set off for the Carbarn, which was around the corner from Heap Square. The Carbarn was like a big garage for trolley cars. Seraphin knew what awaited him there. He would ask the cashier, "Could I have five dollars in change? It's for Joe the Cobbler," and the cashier, a dour, bald guy, would give him a disgusted, withering look, which was humiliating, but he would give Seraphin the change, and that's all that really mattered.

Seraphin liked going on jobs for Pa. It showed Pa had trust and confidence in him, letting him carry five dollars around.

CHAPTER 2

GRAPES

Pa had wine on his mind. Seraphin knew because Pa started asking Laura how much the grapes were at her store. Pa knew her store would sell them the cheapest. Pa was interested in the small green seedless grapes. He didn't want the big purple ones that had seeds.

He asked her the price per pound and she told him.

"Too much," Pa said, shaking his head. "Too high."

"Well, don't give me heck about it, Pa," Laura said. "I'm not the one who sets the price."

"Every year the price goes up," Pa complained. "Three years ago you could get all the grapes you wanted for seventy-five cents a box, and they were happy to get rid of them. Now this year it's going to be at least a dollar a box."

"The price will come down later," Laura said.

"I know that," Pa said, laughing. "That's what I'm waiting for."

A couple of days later he asked Laura the price again.

"Oh, man, why don't you let the poor girl alone?" Ma said. "She doesn't need you to be pestering her all the time about the price of grapes. Do you think they change the price every day?"

He turned on Ma sharply.

"This is between me and her," he said. "Why do you have to stick your nose into everything?"

On Sunday Pa asked Laura the price again.

The trick was to buy the grapes on the right Saturday. It had to be a Saturday, because Sunday was the only free day Pa had to squeeze them. The trick was to guess when the peak of the harvest was coming, because then the grapes would be at their most plentiful, and therefore at their cheapest, and also at their sweetest. If you waited too long, you missed the peak, and then the price went up again. That was what was driving Pa crazy, trying to guess the right moment to buy.

The following Wednesday Pa asked Laura again. She told him.

"The price has dropped!" he said. "I am not going to wait any longer! I am going to buy the grapes this Saturday! I will see the Jew tomorrow morning and give him the order."

Thursday night Pa came home very happy. "I saw the Jew this morning. He gave me a good price. One dollar a box. I was willing to pay a dollar-fifteen a box, but a dollar a box is even better. I'm very content with that price. This year I'm going to buy five boxes. Last year I bought four boxes. But this year one more box! I'm going to pick them up Saturday night."

"I don't know why you bother," Ma said. "To waste all that time and money. What for? To make vinegar. To him it's a special wine. Better than the store sells, he says. But to everybody else it's vinegar."

"Ssshhh, woman. Why do you concern yourself with this?"

"A wine so special that only he knows how to make it. A wine so weak even a baby could drink it without any ill effects!"

"Always has something to say," Pa said. "She is small but she makes much noise. Enough for fifty like her."

"Donkey piss! That's your special wine. Who is it that will be fool enough to drink it beside you?"

Pa was furious.

"Did I ever ask you to drink any of it?"

"Ask me all you want! I wouldn't drink any of it, even if you paid me!"

Seraphin was not looking forward to Sunday. He would have to spend the whole day down cellar squeezing grapes into pans with Pa. And Pa was so fussy. Seraphin would squeeze a handful of grapes till the last drop was out and would try to discard the pulp, but Pa would say, "No. There's a lot more juice in that. Squeeze some more." The sticky juice would run down his arms. And from the weary, monotonous, hard squeezing, handful after handful, all day long, his wrists and fingers would ache. And worst of all—the itch. Halfway through the day, the palms of his hands and his fingers would begin to itch, with a deep, crawling itch that seemed to come from underneath the skin, so deep that scratching did not help. His fingernails could not reach the itch. And his back would ache from being hunched over. Little tiny fruit flies would buzz around his face and he couldn't brush them off because his hands were wet with the juice. No, he was not looking forward to Sunday at all.

Saturday night they heard the screened entry door downstairs close quietly and then coming up the stairs Pa's footsteps, quick and soft. He was in a hurry. Usually on a Saturday night, his footsteps were slow. Also he was coming home one hour earlier than his usual Saturday-night time of midnight.

The door opened and there he stood, blinking in the sudden bright light. His bloodshot eyes were popping out of his head with fatigue. He looked like a coal miner. His face and hands were black. He had no running water at the shop to wash, and during the day the dirt from the shoes mixed in with black shoe polish and dye and somehow it got all over him.

"What have we here?" Ma hailed. "A beast from the swamp. A man so filthy that he fills you with horror."

Pa set down his dinner bag on the floor by the wall. He was not too tired to notice a dollar bill lying on the sink counter.

"You shouldn't leave money lying around," he admonished Ma. "If this was on my counter in the shop, it wouldn't last two minutes."

"I didn't expect there would be a crook hopping around in my house," Ma retorted.

"It's your house, but still, you shouldn't leave money lying around."

"Well, if it's missing, I'll know who took it," Ma said.

"I'm going to the Jew," Pa said. "To get my grapes."

"Sit down and eat a little something first, man."

"No. He closes at midnight. I don't want to miss him."

"You have a lot of time to midnight yet. Sit down."

"No. When I come back, then there'll be plenty of time to eat. Seraphin, do you remember where I put that big piece of rope? The old clothesline?"

"It's in your closet in the box of tools," Seraphin said.

"Oh, yes. Good. Go get it for me."

Meanwhile Ma had gone over to Pa's dinner bag on the floor.

"Your whole dinner is here!" she exclaimed, horrified. "You didn't eat anything! Are you crazy? Are you trying to kill yourself?"

"I was too busy. I can't eat with the shop full of people. I have to be alone to eat."

23

"You haven't eaten anything since six o'clock this morning. You're going to kill yourself, that's what you're going to do. Look at yourself— so skinny! Do you want to get tuberculosis? What good will the money do you when you're dead?

"I ate the bread anyway," Pa said.

"Bread," Ma snorted scornfully.

Seraphin handed Pa the rope.

"Seraphin, I want you to go down cellar and get your team and meet me outside," Pa said.

"Okay, Pa."

Seraphin went down the stairs to the first floor, then along the short hallway to the cellar door. Then down some more stairs. It was pitch-black. He went slowly, feeling his way. The cellar stairs and the cellar did not have any electric lights and Pa did not have a flashlight. He could have gotten a candle but he didn't want to do that. Besides, how could he carry the team with one hand?

He made it off the last step without mishap. He was now in the cellar. It was scary. He was always afraid someone was waiting for him in the dark, waiting to reach out and grab him. He took his outstretched arm and felt in front of him, beside him and behind him. Nobody.

It was scary. But it was fun, too. Like being blind. In the blackness he had his hands out, feeling his way. And there was a lot of junk all over the place in the cellar. But he knew where everything was. He did-n't bump anything. He went straight to his team, picked it up, and carefully made his way across the floor and up the narrow stairs.

This was a great team. It was shiny and streamlined, with a wooden body. It was painted a bright yellow, and on each side in bright red let-ters was its name, *Night Flyer*. And could it ever go! It had real ball-bearing wheels, even though they needed some oil, if he could get some oil someplace. Of course, he didn't use it as much as he did when he first got it. But this team was the best Christmas present he had ever got. Ma gave it to him. She paid two-fifty for it at Ralph's Bird Shop.

Pa was waiting for him out on the sidewalk. Pa dropped the rope on the team. "This is to tie the boxes down," he explained. They walked along side by side, Seraphin pulling the team by the handle. Of course, if he had been alone, he would have ridden the team, pumping with his left leg.

"Tomorrow we make the wine, Seraphin!" Pa announced happily. "Tomorrow we make the wine!"

Now that they were actually on their way, Pa was in high spirits. He walked along with a quick and energetic step. He was gay, almost elated.

"We're going to make some nice wine, Seraphin. Then in the middle of the winter, when you're cold, I will give you a little glass. It will warm you right up."

"Yes, Pa."

"You drank some last year, Seraphin. It was good, wasn't it?"

"Yes, it was very good," Seraphin agreed loyally.

"There's something about your own wine," Pa said. "I don't know what it is, but to me, your own wine always tastes better than the kind you buy in the store."

"Yes, Pa."

They came to the alley that went behind the Old Colony Fruit Store. This was where the trucks unloaded. At the entrance to the alley, Pa said, "You wait here. He will have the boxes by the back door. I will go around through the front and tell him I am here."

Seraphin sat on the team and waited. It was a nice night, not terribly hot like some of the nights had been lately.

In a very few minutes, Pa was back. His eyes were bright and his jaw was set.

"Come on, Seraphin," he said. "We're going back home."

"What about the grapes?" Seraphin blurted out.

"There are no grapes," Pa said.

And on the way home Pa didn't say another word.

Seraphin kept his pace to Pa's and Pa was now walking much slower. In fact, he was really dragging. And Seraphin noticed a big change in his face. Before, when he was happy, he hadn't looked tired or dirty. He kind of shined. But now his face was lined with fatigue and he looked terribly dirty.

When they got home, Seraphin didn't take his team down cellar. He didn't want to go through that again. He put it in the back yard. It would be safe there until morning. And he carried the rope upstairs.

Pa was washing his hands in the sink, scrubbing them with the Octagon cleanser powder.

Ma was getting his supper ready.

25

He still hadn't spoken.

He sat down at the table and Ma set a plate of soup and a spoon before him. Then she brought over half a loaf of Portuguese bread on another plate. As he ate the soup, every now and then he would tear off a chunk of the bread with his hands and eat that.

"So? Where did you put the grapes? Down cellar?" Ma said.

He did not answer, so she knew something was wrong.

"When you don't want to hear him, he talks a mile a minute," Ma said. "But when you ask him a question, he won't answer. Talk, man. Say something."

"There's nothing to say."

"Where did you put the grapes?"

"I have no grapes?"

"You have no grapes?"

"No. I have no grapes."

"What happened?"

"That accursed Jew . . . that son of a whore . . . he sold them to somebody else. He tried to put the blame on the boy. He said the boy sold them. But I could tell he was lying, the way he was looking at me. He wouldn't look me in the eye. He kept looking away from me."

"Maybe he just forgot about you."

"Forgot about me? Hah! Forgot shit! I know that man. He forgets nothing when it comes to money. I know what happened. Somebody came in and offered him more money. And he said, 'Sure, take them.'"

"Maybe he didn't think you would show up, and the grapes would spoil."

"He knows me! He knows I show up! I have bought grapes from him for the past three years. He knows I'm good for the money. And I told him Thursday morning—'Do you want me to give you some money now?' And he said, 'No, that's okay. I know you're all right.' He's a scoundrel, that's all."

Pa ate in silence for a while but he could not long contain himself. "This is insufferable!" he cried. "I close my shop early. I come running home for this. The Jew did a good job on me there. Oh, yes, a very good job. He played me for a fool. That son of a whore. What's his name, Laura?"

"Benny."

"Yes. That Benny. Those grapes belonged to me! He shouldn't have sold them."

"And I suppose you wouldn't have done the same thing," Ma said, "If someone had come to you and offered you more money, you wouldn't have sold them to him."

He turned on her angrily.

"What do you take me for—a piece of shit? If I give somebody a price, that's the price. I don't go changing it! I don't care if I lose money on it or not!"

Pa chewed thoughtfully on a piece of linguiça that had been in the soup. Then he started up again.

"You can't trust the Jews. And they are all religious. Every last one of them. They are all afraid of dying. Even the biggest crooks among them are religious. But I think in their religion, they can't cheat each other. But if a person is not a Jew, him you can cheat."

Seraphin was secretly very happy. He was thinking: Boy, I won't have to spend all day Sunday squeezing grapes.

27

CHAPTER 3

THE RIDE OUT

They ate supper early on Sunday night as usual and afterwards Seraphin went and sat on the steps of his front piazza. It was a little after six o'clock, the end of a lazy, sun-filled afternoon.

Sundays were so dead. The street was deserted. The kids didn't play games in the street that day. Everybody disappeared. And when you did see somebody, young or old, he would be going someplace special, dressed in uncomfortable new clothes and tight shoes, and just seeing him would make you feel sick.

That was why Seraphin was glad when Mr. Patnaude, a bald-headed wisp of a man, came by, because Mr. Patnaude was dressed in the same shabby gray suit he wore during the week. Mr. Patnaude always had a very preoccupied air about him and he didn't look to the right or left as he took his short, quick steps on his way home. Years before Mr. Patnaude had worked in the cotton mills, they said, but ever since Seraphin knew him he had been an inventor. At least that's what the kids said he was. They said he had invented a perpetual motion machine. Anyway he was always in a hurry. And his daughter worked in the sweatshops.

After Mr. Patnaude, nobody came by for a long time. And there were no cars going by. It was really a dead, dead Sunday. Then Seraphin saw Chimp Silva coming down the street from his house. Chimp was in the same grade Seraphin was, but he was older. He had stayed back twice. He wasn't good at school work but he was a real success outside of school. He had energy and nerve. He got jobs. All the kids envied him because he helped clean up the Grand Theatre every morning during the summer and on Saturdays and Sundays during the rest of the year. For that he was paid with free passes and they gave him the stills they put outside in the glass cases to advertise the movies showing inside. Chimp had a huge collection of these stills, all the cowboys, Bob Steele, Hoot Gibson, Buck Jones, Jack Hoxie, Tom Tyler, Buzz Barton, Ken Maynard. And on the Saturday night before Easter, Chimp got to ride up front with the driver in one of Shank the Florist's trucks, and Chimp would run up the stairs into the houses, delivering flowers all over the city, until midnight. For this he was paid money.

Like Seraphin, Chimp was not dressed in his Sunday clothes. He came striding down the street, his chest swelled up with aplomb and verve. Then he saw Seraphin. He crossed the street and came over to Seraphin's piazza.

"Whattaya doin', Seraphin?" he greeted him cheerily.

"Nothin'."

"You wanna come with me?"

"Where?"

"Riding the streetcars. I got two Sunday passes."

Seraphin's face showed his excitement.

"Gee! Sure! But I'll have to ask my mother first."

"I'll tell you what we'll do. I'll take you downtown and then we'll catch a bus to Ossawona."

"Where's that?"

"That's out of town."

"Out of town? Gee! I've never been out of town!"

To leave Gaw! What an adventure!

"Wait for me, Chimp! I won't be long!"

Seraphin got up and ran up the stairs.

This was going to be the tough part, convincing Ma to let him go. The Sunday passes cost twenty-five cents each and they permitted you to ride anywhere on any streetcar all day long on that particular Sunday, even back and forth if you wanted to, from one end of the city to the other. But Ma would want to know how Chimp had gotten hold of two passes. Certainly he hadn't paid for them. What could he tell her? And another thing, he certainly wouldn't tell her he was going out of town. That would just scare her and she would be certain to say no.

Ma didn't like Chimp. She didn't trust him. And she felt he was low class. Ever since Chimp had been sent home from school with bugs in his hair, she had felt that way.

He opened the door and went in. Ma was sitting by the window. He tried to speak matter-of-factly, calmly, like it was nothing.

"Ma, one of my friends has two Sunday passes and he invited me to go with him for a ride. On a streetcar," he finished lamely.

Ma frowned suspiciously.

"Which friend?"

"Chimp Silva."

He held his breath.

"That one, huh?" she snorted. "Where did he get two Sunday passes?"

"I don't know."

"Probably stole them!"

"I don't know, Ma. Maybe his mother and father bought them."

31

She snorted again. "The Silvas have no money for Sunday passes, Seraphin! They barely have enough to eat!"

Seraphin waited.

"Where would you go?"

"Downtown."

"What for?"

"Just to see the sights."

"There's no sights there! Everything's closed."

Pa broke in. "Let him go, woman. He's old enough."

She turned on him in a fury.

"This doesn't concern you! Just because you spend your whole life down there with all those bums and riffraff in Heap Square, you want him to be a bum too?"

Pa began to laugh.

"Those bums and riffraff paid for that chicken that is laying so nicely in your stomach right now!"

"He's my son!"

"True," Pa said, nodding ruefully. "But you forget—he's my son, too."

"All right, boy," Ma said. "You go. But don't come home too late."

"I won't. Gee, thanks, Ma!"

"One thing, Seraphin," Pa said. "Don't you get off that car, do you understand? Wherever the car goes, it always comes back. So you stay on it and you won't get lost."

"Okay, Pa, thanks."

He dashed for the door.

"Have a good time, boy!" Ma yelled after him down the stairs.

"Okay, Ma! Thanks!"

Chimp was waiting for him.

"Okay, Chimp, I can go," he announced happily.

They set off down the street.

Seraphin wondered if they would get an open summer streetcar or a closed winter one. He hoped it would be an open one. He loved to watch them go by. He loved to watch the fare collector hang on with one hand and swing out over the street, going from row to row, while the car was moving. It looked like such an exciting and dangerous job. When he was a little kid he used to set up chairs in a row and pretend he was the fare collector. He'd grab an imaginary overhead bar and swing in and out. Then at the stops after the last person got on, he'd pull the cord and imitate the sound, "Ding-a-ling-a-ling," and that was the signal for the man in the front to start up again. Pa said that the streetcar company was replacing the open cars because they required two men to run them and the closed cars only one.

"You never been to Ossawona, huh?" Chimp asked genially.

"Nope. Never."

"You're gonna like it. It's way out in the country. It's not like Gaw. It's real pretty. We'll put the window down in the bus and let the nice cool breeze blow right on us. I go to Ossawona almost every Sunday."

"Wow!" Seraphin marveled.

"Let's go down to the corner of Bullock Street. A lot of people get off there."

That was strange. Bullock Street was not the closest corner that the streetcar stopped at.

"What do we care if a lot of people get off there?"

"Because we have to get two passes."

"I thought you said you had two passes."

"No, I said we're going to get two passes."

Seraphin felt a sinking feeling in his stomach.

"How are we going to get two passes?"

"It's easy. You'll see."

Seraphin had some faith in Chimp, but he felt very uneasy.

They stood at the corner of Bullock Street and the Avenue and waited for the next car.

"Here it comes," Chimp announced, as they watched it hurtle noisily along the tracks.

It was a closed car. It was crowded and when it stopped and the front door opened, several people stood in line to get off.

"Just watch me," Chimp said quickly to Seraphin. "I'll show you how to do it."

The first person off was a big man with great big bushy black eyebrows. Chimp went right up to him.

"Hey, mister, can I have your pass?"

"Get away from me, you little bastard!" the man snarled.

There were two young fellows about eighteen years old right behind the angry man. One of the young fellows smiled at Chimp. "You want a pass, kid?"

"Yeah!"

"Here." The young man reached in his back pants pocket and brought out an empty hand with the middle finger fully extended and the two adjacent fingers curled up next to it. He offered the universal sign to Chimp. "Here's your pass, kid." The young man's companion laughed heartily.

People coming off the streetcar were dispersing in all directions. Chimp had to make a quick choice. He chose a husky Polish man with a slight sardonic smile. Chimp walked alongside him.

"Do you have a pass, mister?"

"Yes, I have a pass."

"Can I have it?"

"I paid twenty-five cents for it. Why should I give it to you free? Buy your own."

"But if you're not going to use it any more, what good is it going to do you?"

"How the hell do you know I'm not going to use it any more?"

"Because you're going home."

"How the hell do you know I'm going home? You a mind reader or something?"

"Well, where you going then?"

"It's none of your goddamn business where I'm going."

"Aw, come on, mister. Gimme the pass."

"No."

33

"Don't be that way, mister. You don't need it any more."

"I'm going to tell you something. It so happens I need this pass, but even if I didn't need it, I wouldn't give it to you."

"Why not?"

"Because you're a pain in the neck."

Chimp gave up. He stopped in his tracks and the man kept walking.

"Hey, mister!" Chimp called to the man.

The man turned to look at him.

"Stick the pass up your ass!"

"Come here and say that!"

"Why should I? I can say it from here!"

The man made a move to come after Chimp, and Chimp bolted like a rabbit, with Seraphin right behind him.

The man stood there and laughed and laughed and laughed.

Seraphin was scared at first, then, when they stopped, angry.

"What the heck did you say that to him for, Chimp? What good did it do? All it did is get him mad at us. Suppose he sees us someplace. He could give us a kick in the ass."

"He won't," Chimp said. "We're too small."

They went back to the corner and waited for the next streetcar.

Seraphin was nervous. Chimp got the passes by begging, that's how he did it. And Seraphin couldn't expect Chimp to beg one for him, he had to beg for his own. It would be the first time he had ever done any begging. He felt funny—nervous and yet exhilarated. Of course, it wasn't really begging. It wasn't like asking for money. It was asking for something the people were going to throw away anyway, something they had no need for any more.

Another streetcar was coming. They heard it just about the same time they saw it. They heard the conductor clanging his bell, telling everybody he was coming. It was another closed car.

"All you gotta do, Seraphin, is go up to the person and ask him for his pass," Chimp said. "You saw how I did it, didn't you?"

"Yes," Seraphin said. He was very nervous.

About half-a-dozen people got off the streetcar. Seraphin let Chimp choose his target first. Seraphin was looking the people over, trying to decide who looked like a good prospect. And he didn't have much time. The people were all walking away.

The last one off the streetcar had been a white-haired lady. She looked American. She walked slowly. She was carrying a big handbag made out of straw, with artificial flowers on it. It looked old-fashioned. Seraphin got alongside her.

"Ma'am, are you going to be using your pass any more this evening?" Seraphin asked politely.

The lady smiled at him.

"No, I'm not."

"Would you give it to me?"

"I'd be glad to. I was hoping somebody could get some use out of it. I hate to see things go to waste."

She stopped and rummaged around for it in her handbag.

"My sister gave me hers. Could you use two?"

"Yes, ma'am! I sure could!"

"Here."

"Thank you very much, ma'am!"

"That's all right, sonny."

She smiled at him and went on.

Seraphin ran toward Chimp, who was walking back to the corner with a discouraged look on his face.

"Chimp, I got two passes! That lady gave me two!"

"Jeez! I should bring you with me every time!" Chimp said admiringly.

Seraphin handed one of the passes over to Chimp.

"Thanks," Chimp said.

The streetcar was still standing there, with the door open, even though nobody was getting on or off. The conductor had come outside and had gone to the back of the car to fix something. It looked like he was trying to make a better electrical connection or something. He had a-hold of that thing that went overhead on the streetcar.

"Come on!" Seraphin said excitedly. "Let's get on!" He started for the open door.

"No, no! Don't!" Chimp cried in alarm.

Seraphin came back. "Why not?"

"The conductor might have seen the lady give you the passes."

"So what if he did?"

"I got a pass off a guy once and the conductor saw me get it, so when I got on, he said, 'Let me see that pass, kid,' and I handed it over to him, and he said, 'Here, I want to show you something. You see here where it says *Non Transferable?* That means you can't get it from another person. You have to buy your own. And you didn't buy this one.' So he tore it up into little pieces and kicked me off."

"Gee," Seraphin said in horror.

"So we're gonna wait for the next car. And stand off to one side, don't get near the people getting off. Have the pass in your hand so that everybody will see you have one. The conductor won't dare take it off you then, because how does he know? Maybe your father bought it for you earlier. He could get into trouble, see?"

So they waited for the next car. And they got on. And the conductor didn't tear up their passes. All he did was give them a dirty look. He knew they hadn't bought those passes. But so what? What's a dirty look? It doesn't do any harm. The important thing was they had seats on the streetcar. And then the door closed. And away they clattered. Seraphin sighed in relief. It had taken awhile, but the adventure was finally starting.

Seraphin sat by the window, with Chimp sitting next to him. Seraphin stared out the window, at all the stores going by. They stopped in front of Mrs. Gleckman's. And here Seraphin really stared. He never got a chance to look in Mrs. Gleckman's windows. When he walked by, Mrs. Gleckman was always standing in her doorway and she looked at him hard, like she was thinking, "You filthy-minded sneak, you better not look in my windows." Because she sold brassieres and corsets. Seraphin liked looking at the brassieres. Most of them were very plain, for housewives, but there was always one or two that were different, nice, for a girl in love—lacy things with exciting cups. Seraphin didn't like looking at the corsets. They were wrapped around headless, legless mannequins. They were heavy-duty corsets. Encased in one of them, a woman could safely walk through a hail of bullets. Seraphin couldn't imagine why a woman would want to bind herself into one of those things.

Sometimes Seraphin saw Sydney Gleckman in the store, helping his mother. Sydney was in his class at school. Sydney had no father. He had died when Sydney was a baby. You often saw Sydney walking around after school with his beat-up violin case, going to his lesson. All the Jewish boys went around carrying violin cases. Seraphin was glad he wasn't Jewish. He wouldn't want to play the violin. And he didn't like their food. Sydney ate stuff in his lunch that smelled like fish.

Next stop was the Kosher Meat Market. Seraphin looked at the Hebrew writing painted on the window. What strange letters. He tried to make out what the words said. It was like trying to decipher a code.

They went on. They went through Heap Square and Seraphin looked across the streetcar at Pa's shop, which was on the other side of the Avenue. Then they stopped in front of Silverstein's Furniture Store. A dismal sight met Seraphin's eyes. A young married couple was standing in front of Silverstein's windows. The young man was pushing a baby carriage. The young wife was pointing at the bedroom set in the window, and she was so excited. Her face was lit up and she was talking a mile a minute. But the young husband's face told a different story. He was bored. He was quiet, patient, acquiescent, but clearly bored.

And Seraphin thought with horror: Was marriage some kind of deadly trap? Think of pushing a baby buggy down the Avenue on a Sunday night and standing bored before a furniture store while your wife planned and rhapsodized about some bed. He had seen other young couples like this one. He knew how they spent their time. He saw them walking slowly down the Avenue, stopping before every window, the young wife chatting happily, pointing and commenting on the wallpaper, blankets, gas ranges, refrigerators, toasters, clocks, watches, cups, dishes, hats, dresses, coats, shoes, while the young husband stood in stoic resignation.

Seraphin thought of marriage as being about love, but maybe it was more about buying things. If that were so, what a chilling prospect marriage was.

And if the young couple in front of Silverstein's did not present a dismal-enough picture, there was worse ahead. For soon the streetcar had made its way out of the shopping district of the North End and was now on Pennell Street, going by some old tenement houses. These tenement houses were in terrible condition. They hadn't been kept up. They were badly in need of paint and they had unrepaired broken windows. Pieces of wood had been nailed where the glass panes were supposed to be.

The streetcar stopped in front of one of these houses. A middle-aged Portuguese widow was in the dirt yard, leaning against the gate. She was wearing a black dress. When a Portuguese man died, his wife wore black for the rest of her life.

She huddled against the fence like a crow. In the loose folds of her dress, her body had no curves, no shape, no sex. From the streetcar window Seraphin stared down at her. Her face sent a chill down his spine. Her face was frozen in immobility, staring straight ahead, not even glancing at the streetcar. Her face was set in eternal gloom. No laughter or the hope of laughter would ever crinkle that face. No joy or the hope of joy would ever illuminate that face. No happiness or the hope of happiness would ever glow on that face. The sun would never shine again on that face. A pall settled over Seraphin. As a possibility in life, her face terrified him. The joylessness, the blackness of spirit he saw in that face filled him with dread. He had observed about him that melancholy disposition peculiar to the Portuguese, but that didn't prevent them from laughing. This was something different, something much more terrible and final and overwhelming.

Seraphin's spirits did not revive until the next stop. Then a small man with a funny face and a tall skinny man got on the streetcar together. They looked like Mutt and Jeff. The small man sat behind Seraphin and the tall man sat behind Chimp.

"The first time I saw Hoover was in the newsreels," the small man said. "He came on with his cheeks puffed out like a baby's ass. That should have told me right there."

Seraphin wondered if he had been in the theatre that same night with the man. It was at the Globe on a Friday night. This was two years back when President Hoover was running for re-election. And the show had been crowded and a newsreel was on and they were showing these good-looking guys and girls in bathing suits, racing along the water, hanging onto a rope and standing on a float board, and the rope was attached to a motorboat which was zooming by, and everything was quiet and all of a sudden they showed Hoover seated behind a table talking right at the camera, his eyes blinking, and the whole theatre erupted at the sight of him. Everybody began stamping their feet on the floor and whistling shrilly and Seraphin was afraid they were going to shake the theatre down. He had never seen anything like it. Of course, you couldn't hear a word Hoover was saying, but the second he went off the screen, everything got quiet again. It made Seraphin realize how much everyone hated Hoover.

"Listen to me, Willie," the tall man said.

"I don't think Hoover had the brains to come in out of the rain," the small man said.

"You listen to me now, Willie," the tall man said. "I'm going to tell you something. I'm not going to give you opinions. Anybody can give you opinions. I'm going to give you facts, and you stop me anytime and you tell me where I'm wrong. Okay?"

"The only fact I'm interested in is where to get a job," the small man said.

"Do you know Sol Silverstein, owns Silverstein Furniture in the North End? Now there's one smart cookie, that Sol Silverstein. Well, Sol's brother-in-law, Irving, I was introduced to him. And Irving represents the Corp-o-san Mattress Company. He travels all over the East Coast. And he gets into Washington, D.C. two to three times a year. So he knows what's going on there. We're hundreds of miles away. What do we know about what's going on? You can't trust any of this crap you read in the newspapers. Now he's right there. He goes right to the horse's mouth. He goes to these restaurants where judges, congressmen, senators eat. He listens to them talking. That way he finds out what's really going on. And Irving told me that Hoover had plans on his desk that could have ended the Depression in three months. Hoover called in the heads of General Electric, General Motors, all the big companies, the best brains in the country, and they drew up these plans for him. But here's what you don't know. The Democrats controlled the Congress and they blocked Hoover at every turn, they vetoed everything he tried to do, because they didn't want him to succeed. They wanted the Depression to continue. So their own man would get the credit for stopping it, see?"

"I don't think Hoover could tell the difference between his ass and a hole in the ground," the small man said.

"Now wait a minute, Willie," the tall man said. "I asked Irving, 'How would you rate Hoover as a President?' And you know what he told me? He said, 'Herbert Hoover is the most brilliant President we have ever had, with the possible exception of Alexander Hamilton.' That's what he told me."

"I don't think Hoover knew shit from Shinola," the small man said.

"Well, I'll tell you this," the tall man said. "If the people were smart, they'd vote for a Republican President in 1936. That's the only hope for this country. And I'll tell you why. Who has the money in this country? The Republicans do. And they don't trust Roosevelt and you can't blame them, with his soak-the-rich schemes. So they got their money in hiding. But you wait, the day after the election, if a Republican wins, all that money will suddenly come out. They'd invest it in new factories, produce things, more people would have jobs, it'd be like the Twenties again. It stands to reason. That money is still there. It didn't disappear. People are just hiding it, that's all. But let a Republican win, and you'd see all that money come out again. A country can't get anywhere without the cooperation of the rich, because they've got all the money, and money provides jobs."

"Look! Look!" the small man cried excitedly. "See that flagpole? That's where that goddamn Dago was sitting for eight hours!"

They were entering the downtown district and they stopped by the tallest building in Gaw, the Gaw Hotel with ten stories. It was a horizontal flagpole. It came straight off the Gaw Hotel roof and went out over the lawn in front of the hotel.

"'Give me a job or I'll jump,' he said," the small man continued. "And I looked up at him for five hours. Me and about a thousand other dumb shits. The street was packed from one end to the other. People kept saying he was stupid. But all we got out of it was a crick in the neck—he got a job out of it. So tell me, who was stupid—us or him?"

Seraphin stared at the skinny flagpole. He tried to visualize a man sitting on it, out over space, ten stories up. It made him feel faint.

"It was hot as hell under that sun and we were all jammed together like sardines, hardly able to breathe. A couple of guys passed out from the heat. All of us clowns out there. I got a crick in my neck so bad I couldn't move my head for a week. And this Dago, after he shinnied off the flagpole, everybody cheered, and he must have had a helluva laugh over that. 'Those clowns are cheering,' he must have said, 'and I'm the guy who got the job. I'm the one who should be doing the cheering.'

"The son of a bitch. He's not even from Gaw. He came down from Providence to visit his married sister. He's not even from Gaw. He comes down here and takes a job away from us. The poor fuckin' Gaw workers, you see what sad bastards we are? No jobs, and when one opens up, a Dago comes down from Providence and takes it."

"What kind of a job did he get?" the tall man asked.

"Langevin, the guy who owns Happy Home Bread, offered him a job in his bakery. Langevin heard about it on the radio, so he phoned this priest who was on the roof, and the priest tells the Dago, and he comes off.

"But he had a lot of guts coming here and taking a job from one of us. Don't they have flagpoles in Providence? Why couldn't he jump where he belonged? Just suppose I went to Providence and hung from a flagpole and said, 'Give me a job or I'll jump.' You know what would happen? All those Dagoes would go out in the street and they'd yell up at me, 'Jump, you Irish bastard, jump! Give you a job, huh? What's so special about you? We're all out of work! So jump, you bastard!' That'd be the closest thing to a job I'd get. You see, those Dagoes in Providence, they're meaner than shit. They're not human over there like we are in Gaw. We're tender-hearted. That's probably why that Dago came here—he knew that. He knew we'd give him a job. So what if it's one less job for us. And over in Providence all those Dagoes are laughing at us—'What assholes those Gaw guys are! They give us one of their jobs!' Nice guys get it up the ass every time."

41

"Terminal! Terminal!" the conductor cried out.

The streetcar stopped in front of Prescott's, a big department store. A lot of people crowded around the door of the streetcar, waiting to get on.

"Come on," Chimp said urgently. "This is where we get off."

They followed the line getting off.

"We gotta go to the bus depot," Chimp said.

They walked one block west to a big open asphalt yard. Two buses were parked along the side. There was a small waiting room and people were inside sitting down. Seraphin had never been here.

The destination of each bus was marked on the top in the front in big letters. Chimp went over and looked at the destinations of the two waiting buses. Seraphin followed him. The first bus said Teat's Corner. The second bus said Ossawona.

"This is it," Chimp said. "Let's wait here. We'll be first on." The bus was empty and the door was closed.

They waited and after a while people began to gather behind them. Then when there were a lot of people, the bus driver suddenly appeared and opened the door.

Chimp and Seraphin showed him their passes and they were first on. They had their choice of seats. They both wanted window seats, so they didn't sit together. Seraphin sat on the right side of the bus, about two-thirds of the way back, and Chimp sat by the window in front of him. The bus began to fill up.

Seraphin watched his fellow passengers get on the bus. It was fun to sit back and watch the different kinds of people.

A big fat lady carrying a big package struggled up the steps of the bus. She waddled up the aisle. Seraphin knew she was going to sit by him—he just knew it. She did, taking her share of the seat, plus half of his. He scrunched way over to the side but he still couldn't get away from her. Her bulk overwhelmed him, wedging him tightly against the side, enveloping him, stifling him. He felt like a giant weight was pressing down on him. Just my luck, Seraphin thought, she'll probably stay on the bus all the way to Ossawona.

The fat lady was not alone. Her friend, another lady, had followed her on and sat beside her, across the aisle.

"I didn't know he committed suicide," the friend said.

"Yes, he did," the fat lady said. "That's why they buried him so quick. And they passed him over the wall. He can't go through the gate."

The bus was full. The driver started the engine. The bus slowly rolled out of the yard and headed down toward the waterfront. They went carefully along a narrow, cobblestoned street. The stores here were different than in a regular shopping district. Seraphin studied them all with fascination. The bus pulled over to the curb at the corner. There was a bar on the corner—Dead Man's Anchor. Alongside the bar was an alley. A man was a few feet into the alley. His back was to the bus. He was pissing. You could tell because the alley went uphill. The piss hit the asphalt in front of him and then flowed downhill back on him. That's why he had his legs far apart, so it would flow between them. He must have been holding it in for a long time, because it was making quite a stream.

The sight enraged Seraphin's seat companion. "Look at that, will you? In broad daylight!" Seraphin's window was half-open. She leaned over, squashing Seraphin, and put her mouth to the open part of the window. "Pig!" she yelled at the man.

"Disgusting!" the friend from across the aisle said.

"He oughta be arrested!" the fat lady said. "I'd give him six months in the Workhouse!"

"It's getting so a lady can't walk down the street any more without being embarrassed," the friend said.

The stream began to abate. The man gave his dick a couple of shakes and then put it back in his pants. He buttoned up and then turned around. It was obvious he was drunk. His face was very red and he took an unsteady step. But he was happy. He had a big smile on his face and he gave everybody on the bus a friendly wave. The fat lady had been watching him like a hawk. His smile and wave enraged her all over again. Seraphin could hear her angry intake of breath. Again she leaned over, squashing him again, and bellowed through the open window—"Where was you raised?"

Seraphin would have been interested in the man's answer, but he didn't get the chance to hear it, because just then the bus pulled away.

They went across the bridge. Seraphin loved looking down at the tranquil water and at a small boat that was sailing by.

43

"Jack Doyle came knocking on my door," the friend said. "He wants my vote."

"All Jack Doyle is good for is big talk," the fat lady said. "Especially after he's had a few. But it's all malarkey. When the Hibernians had their picnic, he jumped up on a table and started making a speech. 'If I'm elected, I'm going to do this and I'm going to do that. I'm going to go to Washington and get jobs for all of you!' My husband said he should get one for himself first; he hasn't worked in twenty years."

"But he always dresses so neat. He looks like he has money."

"Yes, he fools everybody. He hasn't got a cent."

"He's a fine-looking man," the friend said.

"Mrs. Doyle told me that when she was in the hospital with her broken leg, he only came to see her twice," the fat lady said. "And when she got home, she took one look around and she could see the place had a woman's touch—everything was so neat, you know. She found out later he had had a housekeeper *living* there—that's what he called her. She was a Polish virgin girl."

It was nice with the window open. A cool breeze came through and hit you right in the face.

Then the fat lady and her friend got off. Wow! It was like a giant weight had been lifted off him. And nobody else got on. He had the whole seat to himself.

They went by a long stretch of woods. It would be an adventure to go exploring in those woods, like he did in the Chace Woods, except that the Chace Woods was very small.

They came to a town. It wasn't like Gaw. There were no cement sidewalks. Instead you walked on a grassy path which ran alongside the street. But walking on this path you would be safe from cars, because the path was built up somewhat higher than the street. There were leafy shade trees along the pathway. And the homes were set back quite a ways from the street and they were not crowded close together. They obviously were not tenement houses but were just for one family.

Chimp turned around in front of him. "This is Ossawona," he informed him.

Seraphin nodded.

They came to a corner and the bus swung over to the side of the street, by the pathway. The driver just waited there. No one got on and no one got off. They were parked in front of a house that instantly reminded Seraphin of a book he had read. It was a fairy-tale book and it had wonderful painted illustrations, printed in full color on glossy paper. One of the illustrations was of a gingerbread cottage in the woods and he had spent a lot of time studying and enjoying that picture. It was a magic cottage, and this house was like that. The tenement houses were usually painted a drab gray or brown; this house was painted a gleaming white. The tenement houses all had the same interchangeable vertical oblong windows; these windows were all different sizes. And some of them had wooden shutters. The pitched roofs of the tenement houses always had the same uninteresting, unbroken straight lines; this house had gables shooting off from the main roof, like over a room. It was a magic house.

The house was set way back on the lot, not practically touching the sidewalk, like the tenement houses. There was an immense lawn in front of the house and around the sides and it went all the way to the pathway. The lawn was so green and had been so beautifully tended it looked like it came out of a magazine ad. There were flower beds by the house. There were no fences of any kind.

Seraphin took in the house and the lawn but he took them in as background. What he was really looking at were the people. A father and his daughter were playing croquet on the lawn. They each carried a big mallet and they were making their way through the course, knocking their balls through the wickets set far apart on the lawn. Just as luck would have it, the wooden balls were rolling toward the wicket by the front of the lawn, near the bus. The father was maybe thirty-five years old, good-looking and trim-figured. He was wearing a navy-blue blazer, vanilla-colored flannel pants, and absolutely immaculate white bucks. He looked rich.

The girl. . . . Seraphin stared at her. He gaped. She was his age. She was the most beautiful creature he had ever seen. Her eyes, nose, lips, chin, neck came together in stunning perfection. Her lustrous soft brown hair came to her shoulders. She was wearing a white dress. She chatted happily with her father. She was perfectly poised. She did not even glance at the bus. Seraphin might as well have been invisible as far as making an impression on her consciousness went.

A beautiful girl playing croquet on a green lawn. He knew who she was. She had stepped out of the billboard on his corner. She lived in the world of The Pause That Refreshes. After this game, she and her father would sit on the front porch and have a Coca-Cola.

He had never had a Coca-Cola. He often wondered what it tasted like. The Coca-Cola Company seemed to own the billboard on the corner. Every few months they put up a new ad on the billboard. The billboard was on the side of the grocery store so it was at ground level. That way you could see it good. And the ads were always the same. Beautiful girls laughing and having a good time and looking right at him. And he looked right back at them. Hundreds of times he looked back at them. Beautiful girls. Blondes, brunettes, redheads. In their white shorts by the net, taking a break from the game, a tennis racquet in one hand, a bottle of Coca-Cola in the other. In their bathing suits, by a little driftwood fire on the beach, at a wienie roast, a hot dog in one hand, a bottle of Coca-Cola in the other. In a brown autumn sweater, in the stands at a football game, a pennant in one hand, a bottle of Coca-Cola in the other. And always close by them, their boyfriends, clean-cut and handsome, smiling and laughing, too. Everybody having a good time, doing the things Americans did, the way Americans did them, with that maddening easy acceptance and casual confidence.

He heard the laughter of the girl and her father. They were enjoying themselves. He saw the easy camaraderie of the father. He knew he was looking at the real Americans. He knew that he was looking at the real America that lay just outside of Gaw. The girl lived in that world, a world of ease, pleasure, joy, leisure, gratification, luxury, happiness. The girl herself was light, airy, bright, and shining. And contrasted to her were the Portuguese girls—with their dark skin and mournful faces, their sad, depressing ways. He did not want a Portuguese girl. He did not want to spend his days pushing a baby buggy down the Avenue and looking in windows at shit. He wanted to blot out of his consciousness that Portuguese face, that widow in the black shroud leaning on the fence gate. He did not want his life to be twisted back upon itself.

He wanted an American girl. He wanted her beauty and gaiety. He wanted an American life. He wanted to play tennis with a tanned girl in white shorts. He wanted to eat a hot dog with her at a wienie roast. He wanted to cheer with her in the stands at a football game. He wanted to carry her books home from school with the leather strap around them and then have a Coca-Cola with her on the front porch. He wanted an American girl.

And here was the girl. Here was the girl he was in love with. His eyes never left her face. She was so close. He could almost reach out and touch her. She was so lovely. It was like watching a beautiful actress in the movies.

Her beauty was radiant. His yearning for her was total. And as he memorized her face, he felt a sharp pain. For he knew the truth. She would never be his. For besides beauty, she radiated poise, superiority, impregnability. She was just a few feet away from him but the distance was unbridgeable. She would never love him. She would not waken to his kiss, as in "The Sleeping Beauty," a story he often dreamed about. It would be more like "Beauty and the Beast," except that as the Beast he would be forever repugnant to her. He would never carry her books home from school. It would take an All-American boy, a football hero with a big school letter on his sweater, to do that. He was a Portagee. He was not an American. He did not belong in any scene from The Pause That Refreshes. He could not banter effectively at the net or cheer convincingly at the game. She would quickly find him out. She would know he was a fake, an imposter. In fact, he knew that even if he had a Coca-Cola someday, it would not taste as good to him as it did to the Americans, because by all that was proper and right, he was not supposed to drink it.

The bus started rolling. They were being parted. He was wild with loss. He wanted to yell at her, to let her know how much he loved her.

But it would not do. He must disappear without giving her any sign of his existence. He watched her recede in the distance until he could see her no more.

He sighed. How sad love was. He did not even know her name.

Maybe her family would move to Gaw. Maybe she would live on his street. He would take her blueberrying in Chace Woods. He would show her where the stone tunnel was that went under the railroad tracks. They would crawl in there. It would be dark. She would whisper, "I love you, Seraphin," and they would kiss.

Chimp turned around in his seat.

"How do you like Ossawona?"

"It's nice."

"I told you you'd like it," Chimp said.

47

CHAPTER 4

JIMMY

Pa came home from the shop all agitated. Usually he came home tired and quiet and washed his hands right away and sat down to eat his supper. But tonight he was too upset to sit down. He walked back and forth.

"That Jimmy!" he cried. "That son of a whore! He did a good job on me tonight!"

"What did he do—steal your roll?" Ma asked facetiously.

"He cause me a lot of trouble!" Pa said hotly.

They waited patiently for him to continue.

"I can't believe what happened," Pa said, shaking his head. "To think that one minute I was there minding my own business and the next minute I was up to my ears in a dirty predicament. What prompted that big ton of shit to choose me? Why did he have to land on my doorstep? That was one piece of bad luck, I'll tell you!"

"Well, what happened?" Ma asked impatiently.

"I'll tell you what happened!" Pa said. "Tonight about seven o'clock I was working at my machines in the back and I look up and I see Jimmy coming to my shop—he was climbing the steps outside, you know—and so I turned my eyes back to my work—I was sanding this sole—and I kept working—but Jimmy did not come in the shop—and I thought—'Well, he change his mind and went away.' And then I came to the front of the shop and there he was, sprawled on the sidewalk. And he wasn't moving. 'Oh, my God!' I said. 'He has had a heart attack!' You know, Jimmy is a man who is very, very fat and always red in the face. When he climbs my three steps, he's out of breath.

"So I threw down the shoe and I ran outside. 'Jimmy! Jimmy!' I said. 'Are you all right?' And I bent over him. Ah, what a smell of whiskey he had. He smelled so strong he must have spilled some over his clothes. And now he began to mumble to himself. It was no heart attack. He was drunk.

"I tried to get him up on his feet, but he was too big and heavy for me. And he couldn't get up by himself. So he stayed there on the ground. 'This is a fine thing,' I said to myself. I didn't know what to do. If I left him there, the police would come and put him in jail. And I didn't want that to happen to him. So I thought, 'I will get him in the shop and after fifteen or twenty minutes he will sober up.'

"But how was I to get him in the shop? I needed help. This man came by and I asked him to help me, but he only laughed and kept going. Then, lucky for me, MacDonald, the Scotchman who runs the fish market, came by and he knows Jimmy and he help me and we put Jimmy on the chair in my shop. And it was some job. Then MacDonald left and I tried to work, but in a few minutes Jimmy slip off the chair and fall to the floor. And there he was, stretched out on my floor, fast asleep.

"So I said to myself, 'What am I going to do with this guy? I can't let him lie here, because he's not going to get any better. And if I put him outside, in two seconds he'll fall and spit his head open on the sidewalk.'

"Well, I knew he lived someplace on Earling Street, so I thought, 'The only thing I can do is try to get him home.'

"So I bent over him and I started to shake him, to try and wake him up. 'What number is your house on Earling Street, Jimmy?' I asked him. I must have asked him ten times before he heard me. 'Three-five-nine,' he finally said and went to sleep again.

"The upshot of it was that I dragged him out of the shop, locked the door, and started on my way. 'Come on,' I said to him, 'we are going home.' I help him up, you know, and he was leaning on me. Eee, what a weight he was! He makes two of me.

"I got very tired. I couldn't stop to rest, because then he'd fall down and I didn't have the strength to pick him up again. And while I was struggling along, all the people were passing by us and laughing. I don't know how many times I wanted to let him drop to the sidewalk and walk away. I had had enough of this whole comedy in which I had been chosen to play the fool.

"I worked harder carrying him than I had worked all day in the shop. My shirt was drenched with sweat. I didn't think I was going to make it, but finally we got to Earling Street. It's only five or six blocks but when you're carrying a weight like that, each step is an effort.

"But now all the houses were dark and I couldn't see the numbers. Then, Providence, this kid came by on a bicycle and told me what house it was. I took Jimmy there. He lives on the third floor.

"Eee, it was terrible going up the stairs. It was all dark, I couldn't see where I was going. The stairs were so narrow I had to stand behind him and push, push all the way up. And those stairs were very steep, worse than ours. There was danger, much danger, of him falling backwards and taking me with him to the bottom. With certainty, with that mountain on top of me, I would have broken a leg, or worse.

"When we got to the top, the sweat was rolling off my body like I 51 was caught in a rain. I was ready to drop. I had no more strength left and I couldn't talk I was breathing so hard. The minute I let go of him, that Jimmy fell down right there in the hallway.

"I saw this door, with a crack of light along the edges, so I knock.

"I hear this cry from inside, like some angry animal.

"'Who the hell is it?'

"'It's me,' I said, 'Joe the Cobbler.'

"The door opened a little and this wild-haired witch with crazy eyes is looking at me with much suspicion.

"'What do you want?' she said, still angry.

"By now I had had enough of this.

"'I don't want nothing!' I said with some asperity. 'But if you're Jimmy's wife, I got a present for you.'

"Then she saw him lying there.

"'He's drunk!' she said.

"'Yes, I know he's drunk," I said. 'I brought him home for you.'

"'I told him to stay away from you bums!' she said."

"No wonder she thought you were a bum," Ma interjected. "Look at how you're dressed. You're dressed worse than any bum."

Pa ignored that comment.

"She never saw me before in her life," he continued, "and already she was calling me names. What a damn crew the Irish are!

"And then she said to me, 'You got some nerve, mister, getting him drunk, and then showing your face around here!'

"I had intended to help her get Jimmy inside the house, but with this kind of a fusillade, I said to myself, 'You go shit, lady. You get him inside yourself.' And I started to go down the stairs.

"But she wasn't through with me yet. She wanted to give me one more shot. She called after me down the stairs—'You no-good son of a bitch! Don't you ever come round here again!'

"It's true," Pa said in disbelief. "She call me a son of a bitch. I close my shop early, I lose all that time to work, I sweat like a pig carrying that man through the streets, I push him up all those stairs, and for my pay she gives me the thanks of calling me a son of a bitch.

"But I'll tell you one thing. Jimmy can come to my shop tomorrow morning and drop unconscious at my feet. I will not pick him up. I will not move a finger to help him. I will turn my head and keep on working with my shoes. Never again! He can drop dead there for all I care!"

And with that Pa went to the kitchen sink and started scrubbing his hands with the powdered cleanser. Seraphin heard him muttering: "That poor Jimmy. No wonder he drinks. That wildcat wife of his should be locked up in a cage."

CHAPTER 5

HOME FOR DINNER

It was a few minutes past twelve noon, time for dinner. And Seraphin knew it for sure when he heard Laura's feet running up the stairs. Laura worked at the Old Colony Fruit Store and she came home every day for dinner, from twelve to one. The fruit store was close by so she could walk it. Laura worked from nine to six Monday through Friday and from nine to eight on Saturdays. Her pay was eight dollars a week.

Everybody kidded Laura about the rotten fruit she sold and all the flies in the store eating it, but this was mostly because when the fruit got overripe, Benny, the boss, didn't throw it out but lowered the price on it. Benny did a good business because his prices were low and everybody was looking for bargains. Benny owned two Old Colony Fruit Stores, one in the North End and one in the South End. This made it hard on him because he couldn't be in two places at the same time, and as far as supervision was concerned, he felt that when the cat is away, the mice will play.

As soon as Seraphin heard Laura coming, he ran for the door and flattened himself against the wall alongside it.

"Don't do that, Seraphin," Ma said, but she was laughing.

Laura burst into the house and Seraphin simultaneously sidestepped behind her. "Boo!" he yelled as loud as he could. Laura jumped a foot.

"Goddamn you!" she yelled and tried to punch him but he easily dodged it.

"Laura, don't use those kind of words!" Ma admonished.

"Then tell him to quit doing that!" Laura shouted. "I'm sick and tired of him jumping behind me every time I come in this house!"

"Seraphin, don't do that no more!" Ma said sternly.

"Okay, okay," Seraphin agreed.

Laura and Seraphin sat down at the table and Ma bustled around getting the food. Then she sat down with them.

"Well, how did it go today, girl?" Ma asked.

Laura was near tears.

"Oh, Ma, it was awful. I hope to God I never have another morning like this one. Leo got fired."

"Oh, too bad." Ma clucked sympathetically. "He seemed like such a nice boy. Always polite. Not rough like some of them."

"Ma, you know how badly he needed that job. His father's sick and can't work. Leo's got twelve brothers and sisters and he's the only one working. He makes twelve dollars a week and he gives his mother the whole twelve dollars. He's feeding that family, Ma. He's putting the food on that table. And now he's fired. I don't know what that family is going to do."

"Why did he get fired?"

"Oh, it was terrible. Terrible. Terrible. The girls get there at nine o'clock but Leo gets there at eight to open up. But the store's not open to the public till we get there. He usually works around in the backroom till we get there. So we got there as usual this morning, and he let us in. And like usual we got there early, it was before nine, and there were no customers in the place. Well, Leo was in the backroom sweeping, and Helen went back there to sort out the potatoes. And you know the way Leo is. He likes the girls. He likes to flirt and tease. He doesn't mean anything by it. That's just his way. But of course he doesn't do it when any customers are around. So Leo was having a good time telling Helen jokes and Helen was laughing, and there's a cellar underneath the store and you get down to it through a trap door in the backroom, the stairs are underneath the trap door, and all of a sudden the trap door slowly starts raising up like in one of those horror pictures and Helen sees a man's head coming out and she lets out a terrible scream! It was Benny. I ran back there just as he was coming out. What he had done was this. He had come to the store before Leo got there, and he had hidden down there, not making a sound, listening to us, trying to catch us saying something I guess. You see, we're not supposed to talk to each other. And I never do. If somebody asks me a question, I'll answer them. Otherwise I keep my mouth shut.

"Anyway, Benny came out of the cellar. He had been directly underneath the backroom so he heard everything. He was so mad. He was screaming at Leo. You could have heard him out on the sidewalk.

"'For this I made you Manager?' he yelled. 'For you to laugh and play with the girls? You're fired! Get out right now! Take your apron off and get out of here!'

"Leo turned white. I thought he was going to faint. Or cry. Or something. But I have to give him credit. He didn't. He just took off his apron and put it on the pile of potatoes. 'Good-bye, everybody,' he said and he walked out the front door. Three years I worked with him, and he was gone, just like that."

And Laura brushed away some tears.

"We all felt like crying. But we didn't dare. Because if we showed any sympathy for Leo, we'd get fired, too. Especially Helen. She felt responsible. She felt it was her fault because she was the one Leo was talking to. After Benny left, just before lunchtime, she went in the backroom and she stayed there, crying. She couldn't stop.

"As soon as Leo was gone, Benny called us together and gave us hell. 'You girls better start working around here!' he said. 'I don't pay you to sing. I don't pay you to make jokes. I don't pay you to have a good time in this store. I pay you to *work!*'

"I thought, Why is he telling us this? Leo was the only one who liked to sing and tell jokes. And he just fired Leo. The girls didn't do those things. So why is he accusing us?

"And we hadn't had our first customer yet. It was barely nine o'clock. What a way to start the morning, huh?

"And then Benny started in on me. He watched me like a hawk all morning long. As far as he was concerned, I couldn't do anything right.

"Like all those damn Portagee ladies from North Bridge Street. They head straight for me because they know I'm Portagee. So this morning this Portagee lady came in and she's talking Portuguese to me, and I'm talking back to her in Portuguese because she doesn't know any English. And the minute Benny hears us, he rushes over, because he doesn't understand what we're saying and he's suspicious. He thinks we're plotting to cheat him. So he stands right over us, watching everything I do. Well, the lady wants two pounds of peaches. Now you know when you're weighing something heavy like a peach, it's almost impos-

55

sible to make that pointer come out exactly at two pounds. If you were weighing cherries, it'd be different, they're so small. You can take a couple of cherries off or put a couple of them on. You can get it exact. But with peaches, I'd be there all day taking one off and putting one on. So there they both are, Benny and the Portagee lady, watching that pointer. If it's a little over and I give it to her, Benny will be mad. And if it's under and I try to say it's two pounds, she'll be mad. I'm caught in the middle. Jesus, I was a nervous wreck!

"You see, I can't do it Benny's way. He cheats the people by not letting the stuff stay on the scale long enough. He takes it off before the pointer stops. But I haven't got the nerve to do that.

"And then after she left, Benny said to me, 'Talk English to the customers.' But these ladies are from North Bridge Street. All right, I've tried talking English to them. They don't know any English. 'Talk Portuguese,' they say to me, 'I don't understand you.' So there I am. He's there saying, 'Talk English,' and they're there saying, 'Talk Portuguese.' What am I supposed to do? I'm going to end up with a case of ulcers.

"Then this big tough lady came in from North Bridge Street, real brutish, you know the type, kill you for a nickel. I've had a lot of trouble with her before, always complaining about the prices, as if I set them, and she won't let me put anything in the bag without her examining it first. Now we're not supposed to let the customers touch the fruit. If we let them pick out their own fruit, they wouldn't take the fruit with a soft spot or a bruise mark. And we'd be left with stuff nobody'd want. So we have to fill the bag fast and slip in the ones with the bad spots and hope they don't notice. And that's why we hide the bags, so the customers can't serve themselves. Well, just my luck, with Benny there, this tough old wildcat came in and she spotted where we had the bags and she grabbed one and started picking out some peaches—they're on special—and Benny nudged me, as if to say, 'Stop her.' What did he want me to do? Rip the bag out of her hands and have a fight with her right there on the floor? Because, believe me, that's what it would have taken. I said to her in Portuguese, 'Customers aren't allowed to serve themselves.' And she gave me a look that would fry eggs and kept right on picking. And there I was, left standing there sucking my thumb. Then, of course, after she left, Benny gave me some more hell. 'Don't let the customers choose!' Yeah, that's easy for him to say. I didn't see him tackling her.

"Oh, I am so sick of that man. And I'm sick of all the customers, fighting for every penny. And the Portagees are the worst. I'm sick of the whole damn job."

"Every job has something wrong with it," Ma said. "Look at Albertina Braga in the sweatshop. Her boss is over her all day long. At least yours can only be there half the time."

"I'm sick to death of him spying on us, too. He sits in the barbershop across the street with a newspaper covering his face. All you see is his eyes sticking out over the top of the paper. And he's staring at us. Trying to catch us at something. I feel like going over there and ripping the newspaper away from his face and saying, 'Benny, we know it's you.'"

"Maybe the poor man is reading the paper," Ma suggested mildly.

"Nobody reads a paper that way, hiding behind it. And the sheet never moves. No. He's spying on us.

"One day I was picking some cherries from the window counter and a streetcar was going by and I don't know why, but something made me look up and study that streetcar, and there Benny was, in the streetcar sitting by a window, staring at us. Now, Ma, that man has a nice car, a Buick. What's he doing riding a streetcar? He was spying on us, that's what. He probably got off at the next corner. And we know his car. So you know what he does? Helen has seen him riding by in other people's cars, as a passenger, staring in, and going by very, very slowly. You know, nobody drives that slow unless for a reason.

"And when he says loudly so we'll all hear him, 'Well, I've going to the South End store. I won't be back for the rest of the day,' we give each other a look. Because we know, *for sure,* that in about thirty minutes he's going to jump through that door, trying to catch us fooling around.

"You know, I resent it, really. It's an insult. I work hard. I'm not lazy. And the other girls work hard, too. In the busy times, like on Fridays and Saturdays, we're running around there like crazy. The store fills up with people. We have an awfully good business, Ma. You know that. We have the best prices in the whole North End. And people are streaming in and out of there like flies and we're working like slaves trying to keep up. You don't have a minute to catch your breath. And he sees us working like that, and he still treats us like we're trying to put something over on him!

"And whenever he pops in—what's going on? Are we in the back sitting down? No, everybody's working like hell, that's what's going on.

How come we were working? Did we know he was coming in that particular moment? No, we had no way of knowing when he was coming
in. Therefore, we must be working like that all the time. Otherwise he'd
catch us one of those times and he never has yet. And the cash register
is always full. That's the first thing he checks. The minute he walks in,
he goes right over to it and checks it. Well, how the hell did it get full
if we were fooling around? *Who the hell was waiting on the customers all
that time we were supposed to be fooling around?*

"Well, all I can do now, I guess, is grit my teeth and wait for winter. Then Benny will disappear. When it gets really cold, we won't see
him any more. We don't have any heat in the store, you know. Benny
says it's good for the produce. But it's not so good for us. We stand
around breathing out steam and wearing three or four sweaters under
a big coat and two pairs of stockings and shoes and rubber overshoes to
keep our feet warm and with our hands blue trying to weigh stuff. But
the good part is that it's too cold for Benny to hang around. He comes
in, cleans out the cash register, gives some instructions to the Manager,
and leaves, goes back to his nice warm house. But, gee, he sure makes
up for it in the summertime. What time is it, Ma?"

"Relax, girl, you still have ten minutes."

"You know," Laura said reflectively, "That was really a dumb thing
Benny did, firing Leo. I mean from his own point of view. He's only
hurting the store. Because Leo was a very hard worker. Sure, he liked
to have a little fun on the job. Who wouldn't, the hours he worked?
From eight to eight Monday through Thursday, eight to ten on Friday,
and eight to midnight on Saturday. Those are long hours. But there was
this thing about Leo. He might talk to you when he went by or you
went by, but he never stopped working. If he was sorting, his hands
never stopped. If he was sweeping, he didn't stop and lean on the
broom. He kept sweeping. If he was hauling boxes up front, he kept on
hauling. The jokes he used to make, he'd make them while he was
working. He was a very hard worker. And I don't think Benny appreci-
ated it. I don't think Benny ever knew it.

"It's almost as if the harder you work, the less they value you. You
remember Freddie who came before Leo? Freddie was lazy. He was
always trying to get out of work, always complaining, always grum-
bling, always sneaking out in the back alley for a few quick puffs on a

cigarette. And Benny pretty much left him alone. Benny was much harder on Leo than he was on Freddie. I wonder if it was because Benny knew how badly Leo needed the job. Freddie acted like he didn't care what Benny thought. And he didn't. He quit. He wasn't fired. He quit. He could still have that job today if he wanted it. I just don't understand how these things work.

"And you'll see, we'll get another Freddie as Manager. We won't get a Leo. We won't be that lucky. When we girls got swamped up front, Leo would come out from the back and wait on trade. He didn't have to do that. That wasn't part of his job. He was just doing that to help us out, because that was the kind of guy he was. He saw something that needed to be done so he did it. Freddie never waited on trade once in his life. Instead of him doing our work, we had to do his. I can't tell you how much stuff the girls lugged up front when we weren't supposed to—it was his job, but he just didn't keep up to it.

"And now we're going to do a lot more of it. All of it, in fact. We'll have to do Leo's work in the back as well as our own up front. If I know Benny, he won't be in any hurry to hire anybody else. As long as we do the work, he'll save on wages. He did the same thing after Freddie left. He strung us along for a long time, before he got Leo. 'Next week, girls. Next week for sure.' Bullshit. And you know, Ma, I weigh ninety pounds. How am I going to lift up one of those big heavy crates? And a sack of potatoes? It takes two of us girls to drag it and then we're pulling with all our might.

"I'd like to go up to Benny and say, 'What the hell do you think you accomplished by firing Leo? You're not going to find somebody better than he is or even as good. You're going to find worse.'"

Laura shook her head in disgust.

"You know, the thing I liked best about Leo was the way he was, always so cheerful. That's what I'm going to miss the most. On Saturday nights by eight o'clock I get so exhausted I can barely see straight. And Leo has worked just as long as I have, in fact, one hour more, and he will come by and smile and say something funny, like he just started work ten minutes before, and he's still got four more hours to go! I don't know how he did it.

"Well, that's it. He's gone now. No use crying about it. But I'll tell you, Ma, I think I know why Leo really got fired. I think after a couple

59

of years they just get tired of seeing your face around. I really think that's it. It doesn't matter if you're a good worker or not. They just get tired of you. I think that happened to Leo, and I think it's happening to me. I think Benny is getting tired of seeing my face around. I really do."

Laura stood up from the table.

"I've got to go, Ma."

She stood there, thinking, for a moment.

"But poor Leo. Fired just like that. What a shock. Think of him having to go home and give his mother news like that. My God!"

Laura got tearful again.

"You feel sorry for him," Ma said.

"Yes, I do," Laura said. "And I feel sorry for myself. God, Ma, it's a lousy job. I don't know how much longer I can stand it."

Then Laura ran out, down the stairs, back to work.

CHAPTER 6

ON THE BACK PIAZZA

They always had chicken for Sunday dinner, and this Sunday the house was so hot that after they ate they decided to sit on the back piazza where there was a bit of a breeze. Pa, Ma, Laura, and Seraphin, all went out there. They didn't sit on chairs but sat right on the floor of the piazza. Pa was barefoot, but everybody else had shoes on.

Their tenement was on the second story, so their piazza looked down on all the adjoining yards. Their street, Cosgrove Street, was nicer than most streets in the North End. Most streets were solid with three-deckers or three-tenement houses, one tenement to each floor. But their street was mostly two-tenement houses, like their house, and also had some cottages, where one family would live.

There was one such cottage two houses away. It belonged to the German, Mr. Graf. Mr. Graf's daughter had married and moved away. His wife had died. So he lived alone.

Mr. Graf was well-thought-of in the neighborhood because of his garden. In his back yard he had a beautiful garden, crowded with flowers of every imaginable color and shade of color. He also had a small lawn by the garden. On the lawn he had some garden chairs.

From their back piazza they looked down on Mr. Graf's garden and lawn. It was past one o'clock on a Sunday afternoon. Time for the show to begin.

For, as far as Seraphin was concerned, Mr. Graf's back yard was a magic place. The garden and grass somehow changed people, and that was magic.

There were not many German people in the North End of Gaw. But the few there were, found their way to Mr. Graf's garden every Sunday afternoon. They came up the street, one by one. They were older, with gray hair, both men and women. They came in their stiff Sunday clothes. The men's tight, polished black shoes would click on the cement sidewalk. The women wore white shoes. And when they all got there, all five or six of them, they sat down in Mr. Graf's garden chairs. Mr. Graf immediately served them a big glass of beer, the kind of glass with the handle on the side. And then came the magic part. Because, these men and women when they came walking up Cosgrove Street, they were grim-looking, solemn, stern-faced. But once they sat by Mr. Graf's garden, they changed. Their faces changed. Their voices changed. Their very spirits changed. They became alive. They shed thirty years. They told long jokes, both men and women, but only one at a time and everybody laughed heartily at the punch line. They sang songs, sometimes singly, and sometimes all together, a wavering chorus of valiant, cracked voices. They took off their shoes and danced on the lawn, sometimes singly, sometimes all together. The women cackled and played coquette. The men teased. The women shrieked and the men laughed riotously. And Mr. Graf joined in, with his deep voice you could always tell it was him, but he was quite busy fetching them beer from his house. He brought it out in a big pitcher. They spoke only in German but even if you couldn't understand a word, you could tell what was going on. They had fun, and the longer it went on, the more fun they had. Seraphin had never seen any group have as good a time. But then as five o'clock approached, the laughter died down, slipped away, and was gone. And the five or six Germans, men and women, slipped away, too. One by one they left, never together, and back on the street they were again grim-looking, solemn, stern-faced. The garden and the lawn were alone once more. And Seraphin wondered: Did the flowers miss the laughter? Did the lawn find the silence oppressive?

But now it was early in the afternoon and the celebrants were just beginning to intermittently cavort and shriek. The merriment would not reach it's full-throated abandon until about three-thirty.

"The German makes his own beer," Pa said. "Strong, too."

"How do you know he makes his own beer?" Ma asked skeptically.

"Because he showed me in his cellar how he does it. He has several barrels of it. And he gave me a glass. But it was not to my taste. Too strong."

"I think that's very nice of Mr. Graf to invite those people over every Sunday," Laura said. "Not many people would do that, Sunday after Sunday."

Pa broke into laughter.

"Oh, such an innocent you are, Laura," he said. "Do you think the German entertains that rabble every Sunday just for the fun of it? No! Never! He charges them for it!"

"You don't know everything." Ma said. "You judge everybody by yourself. Just because you would invite your friends over and then charge them, that doesn't mean Mr. Graf would do it."

Pa was disgusted.

"I'm telling you—he charges them for it."

"How do you know that?" Ma said. "You can understand German I suppose and you overheard them talking about it. I think you make up half the things you tell us."

63

"I didn't make it up, woman! Crooked Beak came to my shop and he told me all about it." Crooked Beak was one of the participants. Right now Crooked Beak was leaning back and enjoying puffing on one of those tremendously long curved pipes the Germans had brought with them from the old country. "The German charges them fifty cents. Fifty cents and they can have all the beer they want. But before he gives them a drop, he has to have that fifty cents in his hand. You think he's going to give them all that beer free? No, sir! Before they can set foot in that yard—fifty cents, thank you."

Pa's critic was silent before him. Now he could relax and enjoy the breeze. Laura had brought the Sunday paper out with her and she started reading the comics.

Pa cleared his throat. That meant he was about to start in on a new topic. "I'll tell you one thing," he said in an agreeable tone. "We sit here nice, with our bellies full, in comfortable repose, but out there are people suffering terrible things. In my shop I hear stories of such sadness you would not credit them. Do you see that house over there next to the German's?"

"The Wisniewski house. Where Wanda lives," Laura said.

"The very same. Where Wanda lives. Well, I have observed that girl for many years."

"She's hardly a girl," Ma said. "She's at least my age."

"They say she's crazy," Laura said. "She acts kind of funny."

"She's not crazy," Pa said. "She's just timid and afraid of everything."

Seraphin had seen Pa with Wanda in the shop. He always acted very concerned and solicitous with her, like a father with a little child.

"Years ago," Pa continued, "Wanda work in the Conkwright Mill. In the spinning room. And she was a good worker, very conscientious, very fast. Everything was all right, the father was working, the mother was home. But then Wanda got sick. She had—what do they call it?—a nervous breakdown. The boss in the mill gave her more machines to take care of, and she couldn't keep up to them. Her mother told me she wouldn't leave her room. Just sit in the chair there and look at the wall. Wouldn't eat. Wouldn't talk. Nothing. Just sit there. The doctor came and said, 'Put her in Taunton.' Well, the girl wasn't getting any better, so the mother had no choice. She put Wanda in Taunton."

"In the crazy house," Laura said with visible satisfaction.

"Yes, in the crazy house. And there she stayed for four years. After four years the doctor there at Taunton said to her, 'Wanda, you are all right now. You are in as good a mental condition as I am or any person you see walking down the street. But if you go back to working in the mills, you are going to go down again. You'll be back here with us. So you'll be all right if you stay home, clean the house, cook, go shopping, things like that, with no strain.'

"So she come home. Help her mother and father. Then the father die. He left a little money but not much. After a while the money was gone. The mother said, 'I am going to go on Welfare. I need those two or three dollars a week they give you.'

"But the house was in the mother's name, you see. And you can't get Welfare if you own property. She didn't want to sell the house because then she'd have to pay rent. So she decided to put the house in the name of one of her children. Well, she had Wanda there with her. But she didn't have confidence in Wanda. If she put the house in Wanda's name and Wanda got sick again and had to go to Taunton, then the people at Taunton would grab the house to pay for Wanda's treatment. Now the mother had one other child, a boy, Zygie, and it was in his name that she decided to put the house."

"I know him. Zygie Wisniewski. I hate him," Laura said.

"This Zygie," Pa continued, "married a French girl when he was young. But then they got the divorce. He used to go around in his car selling toilet paper to the mills and offices. Toilet paper, paper towels to wipe the hands, things like that. Then this Zygie met a widow. She was more than twenty years older than him. She had a lot of property, many tenement houses left her by her husband. But she wanted to marry this Zygie. So they married. I was told she gave him one thousand dollars on the wedding day. One thousand dollars!"

"Good thing you didn't meet her first!" Ma said, laughing. "You would have done it for fifty dollars."

Pa ignored that.

"The next day Zygie quit work. No more toilet paper. He never worked again. I see him now once in a while, walking around with a big cigar in his mouth. And on his feet he wears yellow shoes.

"Anyway the mother put the house in this Zygie's name and forgot all about it. Then three years ago the mother, old, got sick. She got weak and had to stay in bed. And Wanda took care of her. And the people who saw them together said to me, 'That Wanda is a saint. She treats that old lady so good, Joe. Whatever the old lady wants, Wanda is right there beside her to get it. Always nice to her. Never crabby. Always with patience and a happy face. Dresses the old lady nice. Clean clothes all the time. Feeds her—cuts up the pieces of meat for her—puts the food right in her mouth. And puts the spoon in her mouth with slowness, doesn't fill her mouth up with too much food at a time because she is in a hurry. Then carries her to the bathroom and wipes her behind afterwards.'

"And the mother was there helpless. Wanda could have abused her if she wanted to. But no. That Wanda treated her very good. But the mother die as she had to. This month past she die."

Ma nodded gravely.

"Now when the mother was sick, that Zygie came to see her once or twice a year. He did nothing for his mother. He was waiting for her to die. And as soon as she die, he sent a man over to Wanda to tell her to get out of the house. Zygie has a buyer for the house and the new people want to move in right away.

"So last week Wanda came to my shop. She was over there in my shop, crying, crying, crying. . . . 'I'm going to get kicked out of my house, Joe,' she said to me. 'I have to the end of this month to find a new place. But I don't have any money to find a new place. I don't have

65

any money to pay rent. What am I going to do, Joe? What am I going to do? They're going to put my things on the street.' She was crying and crying there in my shop. 'I'm going to kill myself,' she said. Who knows?" Pa said gloomily. "Maybe she will."

"Poor woman," Ma murmured, shaking her head.

"She was out of her mind with anxiety. Her eyes were those of a desperate woman. 'What am I going to do, Joe? I got no place to go!'

"And what could I tell her?

"So this Zygie," Pa continued, "is going to put his own sister out on the street. And he does not need that house. He has plenty of money. His own sister. Do you believe this? I find it hard to believe. You know, I have no illusions about the human race. I know my customers are trying to cheat me. I expect it. It's a game, to see who will outwit the other person. But this is a different thing. This is his own sister, his own blood. I cannot believe it. He is not a man. He is a monster."

"That doesn't surprise me too much about Zygie Wisniewski." Laura said. "I've always felt that guy was a rat. With some people you can just tell. What surprises me more is that he didn't kick his mother out the day after she signed the house over to him. I'm surprised he had the patience to wait until she died."

"How do you know him?" Ma asked.

"Oh, he comes in the fruit store all the time, Ma. And when he comes in, he always treats me like I'm dirt under his feet. A real big shot, you know, with his nose stuck up in the air. I don't know how many times I've wanted to tell him to his face—'Hey, wait a minute! Your folks came over on the boat just like mine did. So don't try to pull any of that lord and master stuff on me, because I know what you really are—just a big dumb Polock, that's all.' And someday I'm going to tell him that."

They watched the Germans for a while and Laura went back to her newspaper.

"I think I'm going to go in and take a little nap," Pa said.

"Oh, my God!" Laura blurted out.

"What's the matter, girl?" Ma asked, worried.

"Look!" Laura held up a picture in the paper. "Benny. Benjamin Shapiro. He's running for Mayor!"

Pa's mouth fell open. "The Benny from the fruit store?"

"Yes! Benny! My boss! He's running for Mayor!"

"The scoundrel!" Pa exploded. "That he would have the temerity to run for Mayor! That is what is wrong with this country! In this country anybody can run for public office. A person can be an ignoramus, without education, without qualifications of any kind, and he can still run. It should not be allowed!"

"Ha!" Laura said scornfully. "Listen to this—he says he is announcing his candidacy because his friends kept urging him to run. That guy doesn't have any friends. And listen to this—he's going to write a column every Sunday for the *Evening Herald.*"

"The *Evening Herald* is going to pay that dimwit to write a column for them!" Pa began to laugh. "That's too much. The life here in America becomes more unbelievable every day."

"No, Pa," Laura said. "He's going to pay them. It's a political advertisement. He has to pay for it."

Laura read aloud from the paper:

As I See It
by Benjamin Shapiro
There is nothing wrong with our city that a little smile won't help.

"Who wants to hear what that jackass has to say?" Pa muttered. "He is only good for selling rotten bananas."

"He should take his own advice," Laura said. "I don't think I've ever seen him smile even once."

Laura continued to read aloud:

Have you been to City Hall lately to pay your taxes or get a business license, etc.? Did they give you a friendly smile? See what I mean?

"Such effrontery," Pa mused, "that he would offer himself up for Mayor. He has no shame."

Laura read on:

And there's nothing wrong with City Hall that a little hard work won't cure. Last Wednesday an official City car, License 31357, was parked in the parking lot of Cleo's Restaurant from 12:30 to 3:30 in the afternoon. Now folks, the rest of us working people have a lunchtime from either thirty minutes to an hour at the most. Now what I want to know is how come City employees are taking three-hour lunches when the hard-working taxpayers who are paying these City employees' salaries are only taking one-hour lunches at the most? How come, Mayor Mayhew? We simple souls who are not professional politicians would like a straight answer to that.

"That scoundrel," Pa said. "I would not vote for a man who cannot keep his word."

CHAPTER 7

A Loaf of Happy Home Bread

The election was going along fairly quiet. There was an occasional story about it in the *Evening Herald*. There were big posters pasted on the windows of any vacant store on the Avenue, but there weren't too many vacant stores. There were some election cards passed around that ended up in the hands of the kids. These cards were three inches up and down and six inches across and they had the candidate's face on the left side and a few words on the right side. The kids saved them, traded them back and forth, tried to get as many as they could. Also, harder to get, there were round election pins with the candidate's face on them. The kids saved and traded those, too.

Then everything changed when Armand Langevin got in the race. Armand Langevin was French. He owned the Happy Home Baking Company. He was a self-made man, a real success story, one of the few in Gaw in those economically depressed days. When so many other employers were laying workers off, Armand Langevin was hiring. And he did it all with Happy Home Bread. It was the most popular bread sold in the North End of Gaw. Happy Home Bread trucks even took loads of the bread out to the various little towns around Gaw.

The sure mark of Mr. Langevin's prosperity was that he outgrew the building he was renting on Bullock Street and had a brand-new bakery built at the bottom of Cosgrove Street, Seraphin's street. Seraphin had watched it go up, a long imposing two-storied vanilla-colored brick building. It also had a big fenced yard for the Happy Home Bread trucks. It was very unusual to see a building going up in Gaw. When the sweatshops came to Gaw from New York City, they simply moved into the empty cotton mills.

Seraphin had heard of Mr. Langevin but he had never seen him. Then Mr. Langevin entered the race for Mayor. And his face came down on the North End like rain. One day it wasn't there and then suddenly it was everywhere. The face was always the same. It was a side view of Mr. Langevin. It was taken from the left side. He was looking straight ahead and what you noticed was his wavy hair and his jutting jaw. And this face now appeared everywhere. For one thing Mr. Langevin got the great idea of using tenement houses for his advertising instead of just vacant store windows, like the other candidates did. Big posters of just his face and name were pasted on the clapboard sides of tenement houses all over the North End. Also, Mr. Langevin took over the billboards. Seraphin knew of five billboards. Mr. Langevin took them all over. At the billboard by Seraphin's corner, by the grocery store, magnificent waves of hair and a huge jutting jaw displaced The Pause That Refreshes. For the kids Mr. Langevin's campaign was a bonanza. He flooded them with cards. They had never experienced such generosity before from a candidate. Of course, what it actually did was upset the trading market for cards. Everybody had too many Langevin cards. To get a rare card, like one of Benny, you had to trade five Langevins for it.

Seraphin had a stack of Langevin cards. On the left side of the card was his face. Under his face it said:

Armand Langevin for Mayor

On the right side was his message. It said:

Honest
Dependable
Sound Business Judgment
A Proven Success

And Seraphin not only got to read the Langevin message but he also got to hear it. For Mr. Langevin hired a sound truck. He was the only candidate to do so. And all day long this sound truck, which was pasted all over with Mr. Langevin's face, slowly made its way up and down the streets of the North End. Inside the truck the driver, a young man, drove but he also talked into a microphone at the same time. He was clever. When he went down Cupp Street where a lot of French people lived, he spoke in French. But when he came up Seraphin's street where all kinds of nationalities lived, he spoke in English. Seraphin had to marvel at him. He never stopped talking. His voice came out very loud. You could hear him far away. His voice came out weary and rasping and monotonous. He said:

> *"Armand Langevin for Mayor*
> *A Man You Can Trust*
> *Honest*
> *Dependable*
> *Sound Business Judgment*
> *A Proven Success*
> *Armand Langevin for Mayor*
> *A Man You Can Trust*
> *Honest*
> *Dependable (etc.)"*

71

The kids all followed the sound truck, keeping even with it on the sidewalk, because every couple of streets it would pull over to the curb and the young guy would step out and give the kids cards. Sometimes, if they were lucky, pins, too.

But it was really eerie. Because no matter where you went in the North End of Gaw, you could not escape that face. The wavy hair and the jutting jaw. Mr. Langevin looking into the horizon. Sometimes it was a tiny face, as on the round half-dollar-size pins. Sometimes it was a small face, as on the cards. Sometimes it was a big face, as on the tenements. Sometimes it was a huge face, as on the billboards. But wherever you went, that face was there. And then it suddenly dawned on Seraphin. Mr. Langevin was going to win the election. He had overpowered the voters of Gaw. You never saw the names or faces of the other candidates any more. Mr. Langevin was going to win. How could he be resisted?

One warm night, in the twilight, about seven o'clock, Ma turned to Seraphin and said, "We're going to have a treat. I'm in the mood for some nice fresh bread. Seraphin, take this dime and go down to the Happy Home Bread and get me a loaf of bread."

"Do you want the small or the long, Ma?" The small was eight cents, the long was ten cents.

Ma thought for a moment. "Small."

Seraphin was happy to go. He loved making a sandwich of two slices of fresh bread, smeared with butter in the middle. He could eat a lot of fresh bread and he would. Especially since they wouldn't have to save any for Pa. Pa only liked Portuguese bread. He claimed American bread would ruin your stomach. "It's too white," he said. "The flour is no good."

The Happy Home Baking Company was three blocks away, at the bottom of Seraphin's street. But when you were about half-a-block away, you knew it was there. The balmy night air carried the heavenly smell of freshly-baked bread. Seraphin inhaled deeply through his nose.

Seraphin went down a dirt alley alongside the bakery. Toward the back of the bakery he sat down on the ground beside a window. The window, which was small, was positioned close to the ground. To see through it you either had to crouch down or sit down. He preferred to sit. The window was open but it was screened. He was looking into the room where they baked the bread. The floor of this room was not flush with the ground; it had been built below the surface of the ground. So he was looking down at the oven and the two young men working it.

The two young men were French. Even though Mr. Langevin hired more men when he expanded his business, he hired only French, so it was a great piece of luck for the French. But Mr. Langevin's success didn't do the Portuguese, or the Polish, or the Greeks, or anybody else, any good.

Seraphin loved to watch the workers at Happy Home Bread in action. They were so neat and clean. They were clean-shaven. Their hands and faces were very clean. And they wore clean white starched jackets and clean white pants sharply pressed.

The oven room was hot. The two men had stripped to the waist. Sweat rolled down their chests. They worked as a team. They worked as smoothly as a piece of machinery, without hesitation, without stopping.

The oven was a great revolving cylinder. The men would smack open the oven door, reach in, protected by their big thick gloves, and pull out a hot tray of bread and set it on a rack to cool. Standing nearby was another rack loaded with trays that held neat rows of mounds of dough. With expert smoothness the two partners would grab one of these dough trays and shoot it into the vacated slot in the oven. Then they would close the oven door and push the cylinder up, open the next compartment door, get the tray of bread, and so on. By the time they got to their original tray of dough—it was bread. And on and on they went, never stopping. Well, they couldn't stop, Seraphin reasoned, because then the bread would burn. They had to work fast because the oven worked fast.

Seraphin watched the two for a while. He would have liked to stay longer, but he knew Ma was waiting. This was the kind of job he would like to have when he grew up. Working on a bread oven appealed to him. He loved the rhythm of it, the perfection of it, the clean-cut simplicity of it, putting the dough in, taking the bread out.

Seraphin got up and walked around the corner to the front entrance. This was the entrance for the public. He opened the door and walked down some steps. He was in the room where you bought the bread. He walked over to a low wooden railing and watched the most incredible machinery you could imagine. The bread moved along a conveyor belt and first it got sliced and then it got wrapped without so much as the touch of a human hand. At the end of the conveyor belt a man took the wrapped leaves and stacked them in a bread box.

During the day they had two guys in here, one guy to sell the bread and the other to tend to the machinery and stack the bread. But at night because there wasn't much business, they just had the one guy to take care of the machinery and do the stacking. But he was supposed to sell bread on the side, and that was the problem. He didn't like waiting on people because that interrupted his work. He had to rush over to the customer, wait on him, and rush back, while the breads were falling haphazardly into the box. So the night man tended to be a little grouchy. And he showed his displeasure by making you wait a good long time for service, especially if you were a little kid. But Seraphin didn't mind. He was in no hurry. He liked watching the machinery. He was fascinated by the way it sliced the bread and then, maybe even more magical, how it was able to wrap the bread. And so fast. And never a breakdown. Never jamming up. It was mechanically perfect.

But finally the guy came over.

"Yeah?"

"I'll take one small loaf, please."

The guy picked a bread up out of a box he had right by the railing. He handed it to Seraphin and took his dime. There was a cigar box with some change in it sitting on a chair. The guy dropped Seraphin's dime in the box and took out two pennies. He gave them to Seraphin.

"Thank you," Seraphin said.

The guy didn't say, "You're welcome." He just rushed off to stack the bread.

Seraphin put the two cents in his pocket. He shifted the bread from his left hand to his right hand, being careful not to hold the bread too tightly, it was so soft. He started for the door. When he got to the steps, he noticed his right shoe felt loose. He looked. The lace had become untied. He set the bread down on one of the steps and bent over to tie his shoe.

Then it happened. So fast, he didn't have a chance to say, "Watch out!" or anything. The door burst open and a man hurriedly came down the steps. Seraphin watched in paralyzed horror while a great big heavy leg with a big black shoe at the end of it came down squarely on top of the middle of his bread. Seraphin stared at his bread in open-mouthed shock. The bread was crushed, smashed, destroyed, demolished. The wrapper was torn and dirty from the shoe. What had been a perfect brand-new loaf of bread was now deformed beyond reclamation.

The heavy feeling in the pit of his stomach told him he was involved in a disaster. What would Ma say? How could he possibly explain it? It was all he could do not to cry.

As for the man replacing the loaf, he knew he was out of luck. It was his fault for placing it on the step. Nobody in Gaw would buy him a new loaf. They would say, "Tough luck, kid," and laugh. And he had already paid for it, so the bread man wouldn't give him another one.

Then he looked up at the man. The same wavy hair. The same jutting jaw. Although he was now wearing gold-rimmed glasses. And the jaw didn't jut so much. There could be no mistake. It was Armand Langevin. Seraphin felt like he was looking at a movie star. Somebody famous. He felt awe.

Armand Langevin bent over and picked up the sorry loaf. He was laughing. He took it over to the railing. "Here, Hector, take care of this. And give me another loaf."

Armand Langevin took the new loaf over to Seraphin, who hadn't stirred from where he had tied his shoe.

"Here you are, son," Mr. Langevin said with a friendly smile and handed Seraphin the bread.

"Thank you," Seraphin said, looking him in the eye.

Seraphin went up the steps and out into the fresh air. He was in a glow. What a guy that Armand Langevin was. He was the only guy in Gaw who would have replaced the loaf. It was so totally unexpected. Seraphin had been sure that a disaster had happened and that it would remain a disaster. But Mr. Langevin had fixed it all up, like it had never happened.

Seraphin was elated. He had escaped. Of course, he wouldn't tell Ma what had happened. She would give him hell for being stupid enough to put the bread on some steps.

But he couldn't get over that Mr. Langevin. What a swell guy. Boy, he really liked him. If he could vote, that's who he would vote for. He sure hoped that Armand Langevin would win the election.

75

CHAPTER 8

His Honor the Mayor

Seraphin got to the French pastry shop at about twelve-thirty. He bought two turnovers, one strawberry and one lemon. They were two for five cents. He put the little white bag with the turnovers in the leather bag that held Pa's dinner. Both turnovers were supposed to be for Pa, but Pa was real nice. He always gave Seraphin one. That was why he had bought the lemon one. If he was going to get one, he might as well get the flavor he liked, and he loved lemon. Mmmm, a flaky, delicious lemon turnover.

Mrs. Pittsley the Communist was just leaving when Seraphin got to Pa's shop. Mrs. Pittsley stood in the doorway. Her eyes were bright with the fanatic's fire.

"They're building a new world over there, Joe!"

"Where?"

"In the Soviet Union!"

"You going to go there?"

"There's no bread lines in the Soviet Union, Joe! Everybody's working there!"

"You going to go there?"

"There's justice for the workers over there!"

"You going to go there?" Pa shouted, exasperated.

"No, why should I? I'm not Russian. But that's no reason why I can't admire the achievements of the Russian people!"

"It's heaven for the workers there?"

"That's right, Joe! It's the workers' paradise!"

"I'm going to tell you something. I don't believe in paradise on this earth. Paradise comes after you die, when the angels come down and get you," Pa said with a sardonic laugh.

"That's superstition!" Mrs. Pittsley said. "But I'm late for work, Joe. I'll be back Saturday for the shoes."

"Yes," Pa said.

She left, and Pa turned to Seraphin, shaking his head.

"That woman is a fool. It is strange but there are people who cannot learn the lessons life teaches. They are born a fool and they die a fool. Paradise on earth will come when we are all saints, and not one day sooner."

Seraphin had put Pa's dinner at the back of the shop. Pa's shop was small—narrow and not deep. It did not have a backroom, so Pa had to eat in plain view of his customers, which he did not like. Of course, even if he had had a backroom, how could he have eaten there and left the front unattended so that things could have been stolen? Pa always sat on the stool by the sewing machine, which was toward the back of the shop, and ate there. Pa didn't have a toilet or running water either. He couldn't wash his hands during the day and to pee he filled a malodorous bottle behind the counter.

"I've got a job for you, Seraphin," Pa said. He pointed at a carton on the counter. "I just got a shipment of heels from Goodyear. Count all the boxes and tell me how many boxes there are. I want to make sure they don't cheat me."

"Okay, Pa."

He liked counting boxes. He liked the strong rubber smell of the heels and he liked the crisp, clean newness of the boxes. There was a pair of black men's heels in each box. The carton was already open. That meant Pa had already counted the boxes, so Seraphin knew he was checking Pa's count, but he didn't mind. He started taking the boxes out of the carton and stacking them on the counter in piles of six.

Before he finished, a little girl walked into the shop. She was clutching a fifty-cent piece in her right hand.

"My mother wants her shoes," the little girl said.

Pa turned around and looked at the shelves piled three high with finished shoes and took off his cap and scratched his head in perplexity. He turned back to the girl.

"What's your name, li'l gal?" he asked.

"Yvonne."

"What's your last name?"

The little girl just looked at him.

"What's your whole name? What's your last name?"

The little girl just continued to look at him.

"Don't you have a last name?" he asked in exasperation.

She shook her head.

He took a different tack. "What is your mother's name?"

"Mama."

"This is a fine thing," Pa muttered in Portuguese.

He studied the shelves of finished shoes again and scratched his head some more.

He then looked closely at the little girl.

"Are you French, li'l gal?"

79

The little girl nodded.

Pa smiled. "Ah, I think I know who you are. Is your mother a big fat lady?" and he held his hands way out from his body to illustrate her girth.

"Yes," the little girl said.

"Tell your mother her shoes are not ready yet. I told her Thursday. She come back too soon. You tell her I told her Thursday. Thursday. You understand?"

The little girl nodded.

And then Pa said, taking note of the money in her hand, "Be very careful with that money, li'l gal. Don't lose it. Take it straight home to your mother."

The little girl did not respond to the admonition and left.

Pa turned to Seraphin and complained. "I know this riffraff. I know how they are. The kid loses the money and the mother comes back on me, claims I steal it."

The carton was empty. Seraphin finished his count.

"I got one hundred and forty-three boxes, Pa," he announced.

The self-conscious look on Pa's face confirmed his guess—Pa had already counted them.

"I used one box already," Pa said. "Add one box to your number. Now how many is it?"

"One hundred and forty-four."

"And how many dozen is that?"

"That's . . . uh . . . twelve dozen."

"Good. That's what I ordered. Put them in the window, Seraphin."

The space behind the counter was so crowded with shoes and sup-
plies that the window display area was the only place left to store things.
Seraphin started putting them in the window.

A lady walked by. Her hair was nicely fixed, but it was all white.
And she wasn't that old where she should have had white hair. She was
maybe forty.

Pa pointed at her with his knife. "You see that lady, Seraphin? Too
many permanent waves does that, turns the hair white. Dries the hair
out and then it turns white.

"Now I've got something else for you to do, Seraphin. Take these
shoes to the back and take the heels off them."

Pa gave him three pairs of men's shoes. Seraphin took them to the
back workbench.

It was easy to take the heels off. First you pried the worn heels up
with a screwdriver. Then you pulled the loose heel off with a pair of pliers. And then you pulled the individual nails out of the shoe with the
pliers. Seraphin liked doing it.

Pa picked up a shabby-looking, flat-heeled woman's shoe. He looked
at the sole of the shoe. Then he felt inside with his hand. "It's all rotten
inside," he said disgustedly. "See what they make shoes of today,
Seraphin? Cardboard! Shoes of cardboard! You touch them and they fall
apart in your hands. That's all this is, cardboard. So cheap it doesn't pay
to fix them. You can buy a new pair for the price of repairing them.

"How am I supposed to fix them? How can a nail hold in all this
shit? There's not a single piece of leather in this whole shoe. Shoes of
merda!" He spat disgustedly on the floor and threw the shoe aside.

Seraphin brought up the three pairs of shoes with the heel area
cleaned off and laid them on the counter near Pa.

"They're ready to go, Pa."

"Good," Pa said. "Get me three boxes, Seraphin." And he took the
first pair of shoes onto his workbench.

Just then Alfonso, a mournful-looking, heavy-set, middle-aged
Portuguese man, came into the shop.

"You got my shoes ready, Joe?"

"Yes, yes, they're ready. Come here, Seraphin," Pa said, calling
Seraphin to come behind the counter. "Get that pair of shoes in the
middle there, the brown ones." Pa pointed.

"These the ones?" Seraphin asked, holding them up to Alfonso. Alfonso nodded. He held a dollar out. Seraphin took it.

"How much is it, Pa?" Seraphin knew how much it was. It was just new soles. Seventy-five cents. But he never said the price because Pa didn't always keep to the prices. He sometimes charged less, never more.

"Seventy-five cents," Pa said. He watched Seraphin make the change. Seraphin bent down behind the counter to the iron box on the floor, put in the dollar and took out a quarter, straightened up and handed the quarter to Alfonso. Then Seraphin took a couple of sheets of newspaper and wrapped up the shoes and handed them over.

"How's everything going, Alfonso?" Pa asked cheerily.

"Not so good, Joe. I got troubles. Big troubles."

"What's the matter?" Pa was always very interested in anyone's troubles. You could tell he was very interested because he put down his hammer and gave Alfonso his full attention.

Alfonso sat down in the chair and put the wrapped shoes on the floor.

"Joe, I got a letter from Lawyer Lipschitz. Since I got it, I can't sleep. I can't eat. Worry. Worry. Worry. I'm sick. Lawyer Lipschitz threatens to take me to court. To sue me."

"Sue you? For what?"

"You know that guy Suprenant, the Frenchman who lives next to me?"

Pa looked off, trying to place Suprenant.

"You know the guy, Joe. Tall and skinny. He's always in the barroom. Never pays his bills. They came to his house and took away his bedroom set, mattress and all."

"Yes!" Pa remembered. "He's got red all over one side of his face!"

"Yeah, that's the guy. That's a birthmark. Well, he's suing me."

"For what?" Pa was astonished.

"A week from last Sunday, Joe, I was painting my house. I started off in a bad mood, because I had an argument with my wife. One of the pipes in the kitchen was leaking water all over the floor and she wanted me to fix it, and I didn't feel like it. I wanted to be out in the fresh air. Besides, I had made up my mind to paint. I told her I'd fix the pipe later, so she got all mad, and I got mad, too. So I went outside and I got everything ready. I put up my big ladder on the front of the house. I stirred the paint, got my brush, and took everything up the ladder. So I was up there painting, minding my own business, when along comes that son-of-a-bitch Suprenant.

"He stands right by the bottom of the ladder and he looks up at what I'm doing, and he says, 'Did you scrape those clapboards before you painted them?'

"I looked down at him and I didn't say anything.

"And he says, 'Listen to me now. You've got to scrape the old paint off first. I know what I'm talking about. I used to be a painter. That was my trade.'

"'When was that?' I said. 'You been in the barroom for the last twenty years.'

"He didn't say anything to that, but then after a while he says, 'You don't have enough paint on the brush. Put more paint on the brush and you'll save yourself a lot of work.'

"I didn't answer him, Joe. I said to myself, 'I'm not going to say anything more to him. Then when he gets tired of nobody paying any attention to him, he'll go home.'

"After a minute of two, he says, 'You're not doing that right. You shouldn't paint up and down. Paint sideways. Go with the grain of the wood.'

"Well, Joe, when he said that, all my good resolutions went. I started to get mad. 'Who the hell appointed you boss?' I said. 'Did I make you the boss?'

"It was just like he didn't hear me, Joe. He said again, 'Paint sideways.'

"'I'll paint any goddamn way I please!' I said. 'It's my house, not yours! I'll paint in circles if I want to!' And I was so mad I actually started painting in circles.

"Then he says to me, 'You shouldn't be up there anyway. Don't you know that today is the Lord's Day? You should be in church or resting at home in honor of our Lord.'

"I was so mad, Joe, I kind of went out of my head. I yelled at him, 'I'll give you a Lord's Day!' and I took the paint brush and I put it all the way into the can of paint and then I went like this over his head—" and Alfonso snapped his wrist sharply "—and all this paint went flying off the brush right on him. He didn't say anything. I thought he'd get mad. But he didn't say a word. He just turned around and went into his house. And I thought that was the end of it. Then a few days later I get a registered letter from Lawyer Lipschitz. If I don't pay up, Lipschitz says he will take me to court."

"How much does he want?"

"He wants four hundred dollars, Joe. That Suprenant was dressed in rags, but the lawyer claims I ruined a new suit and new shoes, and he says that Suprenant was put in a state of shock and he had to take to his bed. He almost had a nervous breakdown, and all from five or six drops of paint. Or maybe a little bit more than that.

"I don't know what to do, Joe. I'm getting sick over this thing. I can't sleep. My wife keeps telling me to go see Secundo B. Alves, but I am afraid to. I'm afraid to put myself into the hands of the lawyers. I know them, they will pluck me like a chicken, if not Lipschitz then Alves, or probably, both of them. And my wife says I have to do something for my peace of mind, but I don't know what to do." He put a hand to his head in pain and anguish. "What do you think I should do, Joe?"

"Well, I tell you. I don't think Lawyer Lipschitz wants to take you to court. I think he is trying to scare you. You see, Suprenant doesn't have any money to pay Lawyer Lipschitz. This is a game the two crooks are playing, Lipschitz and Suprenant, to see how much they can get off you and then they split it between themselves. Why don't you go to Lawyer Lipschitz and offer him a hundred dollars, fifty for him and fifty for Suprenant?"

"Lipschitz is not going to be satisfied with fifty dollars, Joe," Alfonso said dolorously.

"Try it anyway."

"Bloodsuckers!" Alfonso suddenly exploded. "If a man has anything, a few dollars in the bank or a piece of property, then those bloodsuckers find you out and come looking for you. An honest man can't sleep nights for worrying. And a bum like Suprenant has the power to torment me and rob me. It's not right, Joe. It's not right. I should have put everything in my wife's name. But it's too late for that now."

Alfonso then picked up his shoes and left.

"That poor fellow," Pa said, shaking his head in sympathy. "He's right. There's no hopes for him. He will probably end by seeing Secundo B. Alves. And when the lawyers have you in their clutches, you might as well hand over your wallet the first thing. There's no hopes for you. They will rob you and what the other lawyer doesn't take, your own lawyer will. They are thieves, all of them. They learn the law so that they can use it to their own advantage. They learn to steal within the law.

"That Suprenant probably had this whole thing planned before-hand. Stand close to the ladder and hope some paint falls on you. But this was better yet. That Alfonso gets mad, falls into the trap, and throws some paint on him.

"I didn't want to tell Alfonso, but the same thing happened to Abie the Mechanic. He had his truck parked right in front of his garage and these kids were jumping up and down on the board that sticks out on the side of the truck. Abie came out of his garage and told the kids to get off. And they did, except one of them, a Polocka kid, a hardened type, he kept on jumping up and down. So Abie went over and grabbed him and threw him off. He didn't hurt him; the kid didn't fall to the ground or anything. But the kid went home, told his father, the father took him to this same Lawyer Lipschitz. Pretty soon Abie got a letter. Lipschitz said he hurt the kid's back, and I saw the kid with my own eyes running around the next day like nothing happened. Lipschitz wanted eight hundred dollars. Abie hired a lawyer, and they settled for three hundred dollars. But Abie still had to pay his own lawyer extra. But the father of the kid, he met Abie one day and he mentioned the settlement of two hundred dollars. Abie told him it was three hundred dollars. So the father got all mad, not at Abie, but at Lawyer Lipschitz. You see, they had agreed to split whatever they got. But what Lipschitz did was tell the father he had settled for two hundred dollars. So he gave the father one hundred dollars and kept two hundred for himself. So the father went all mad to Lawyer Lipschitz's office but he never got another penny from him. One crook stealing from another," Pa said, laughing. "They're all crooks, those lawyers.

"Yes, I feel very sorry for Alfonso. They have him strapped down on the operating table. Nothing can help him now."

Pa then went to the closet at the far end of the counter and brought out an opened copy of the *Boston Daily Record.*

"Here, Seraphin, I want you to look at these dolls and tell me if you see any numbers there."

Dolls was what Pa called the figures in the comic strips. And the *Record* was opened to the *Toonerville Trolley.* Seraphin had done this before. The problem was not in finding the numbers. The problem was that there were too many numbers.

Seraphin took the *Record* and sat down in the chair and studied the cartoon carefully. First, he looked at the cartoon straight. Then he turned the cartoon on its side, first one side, then the other. But, most important of all, he studied the cartoon upside down. You saw some numbers with the cartoon straight, and some numbers with the cartoon sideways, but the most numbers you saw were with the cartoon upside down.

Seraphin studied and studied the cartoon. He went over every single line in the drawing from every possible angle. And he spotted something—a five and a seven close together, in three different places, once in the sky, once in the tail of a horse, and once in the dress of Powerful Katrinka. And then the number three—once in the Skipper's shoe, once in Mickey McGuire's ear, and once in the trolley track.

Pa interrupted his study.

"Eee, the devil!" Pa exclaimed. "Come here, Seraphin. I want you to see something."

Seraphin went over to Pa and Pa pointed at a pair of large black men's shoes on his workbench. "You want to smell something, Seraphin? Smell these shoes." He was laughing and watching Seraphin's face.

Seraphin stuck his nose down by the shoes and inhaled.

If a smell could have a life of its own, if a smell could reach out and slap your face, this one would have. It penetrated right down into your insides. It was an unbelievably powerful, unbearably sour, excruciatingly rancid smell. It made you sick to your stomach.

"Aren't they something?" Pa marveled. "This one wins the prize. They belong to a big Polocka. I guess he never washes the feet. I should charge him extra for fixing his shoes."

"Yes, they smell all right," Seraphin agreed.

"I should take them home and stick your mother's nose in them," Pa said, suddenly grim. "She thinks I'm over here just sticking the money in my pocket. She has no idea what I have to go through for every nickel I make."

Seraphin went back to the chair and reviewed his findings on the *Toonerville Trolley.* He felt confident he had missed nothing. He was ready to make his report to Pa.

He took the cartoon sheet to Pa's workbench.

"Pa, I want you to know I found every number, from one to nine, so no matter which three numbers you pick, they're all here."

"Yes, but were some numbers there more than once?"

"Yes, that's it. Some were more than once. Here's what I found."

Pa was listening intently to him.

"I found a five and a seven, close together, in three different places."

"Close together?"

"Yes."

"That's good! That's good!"

"And then I found a three, in three different places. No other number was there more than once or twice."

"So it was a five and a seven and a three."

"Yes."

"You did good work there, Seraphin."

The *Boston Daily Record* gave you clues like that in every day's paper, but Pa didn't buy the *Record* too often, because he didn't have the time or patience to pour over *Toonerville Trolley*. But when he knew Seraphin was going to be around, then he would buy the *Record*.

"I like the five and the seven," Pa continued, "because they were close together. I have a hunch about those two numbers. Yes, I have a big hunch about those two numbers. The three I'm not so sure about, but I'm going to play it anyway. Five-seven-three, that sounds good to me. But it could be three-five-seven. Or five-three-seven. I'm going to box it. Then I'm protected no matter what."

It cost one cent to play five-seven-three straight, but then you only won the five dollars if it came out five-seven-three. If you boxed it, it cost five cents, but you won the five dollars if it came out with the numbers five, seven, and three in any order.

"I'm going to send you to play this number for me, Seraphin," Pa said. "Jimmy doesn't come by any more. He's got a job now. So I'm going to send you to him. You know on the Avenue near Earling Street where that store used to be selling wallpaper? They went out of business."

"Yes."

"All right. It's a place now where Doyle, that bum who is running for Mayor, has his mug all over the windows. That Doyle rented the store to make the advertise for his campaign. Now Jimmy is working for Doyle. Jimmy stays in that store all day long to mind it, to see that nobody steals anything. He opens it in the morning and closes it at night. He sweeps it and keeps it clean, things like that. So he will be inside that store.

"Now listen carefully, Seraphin. Don't go in there if somebody is with Jimmy. Only go in there if he's alone. You understand?"

"Yes. Only go in if he's alone."

"Yes. Tell Jimmy I want five-seven-three, boxed."

"Five-seven-three, boxed," Seraphin repeated.

"Yes. Five-seven-three, boxed."

Pa went down to his money box on the floor behind the counter and came back up with a nickel, which he handed to Seraphin.

"Oh, one thing," Pa said. "If you see Frankie the Midget, you can give him the number and the money. He's just as good as Jimmy."

"Well, which one would you rather have, Pa?"

"It doesn't matter. Either Jimmy or Frankie, either one is as good as the other."

"Okay, Pa. I'll be right back," Seraphin said, and off he went.

He did not dawdle but marched right along and in a few minutes he was by Earling Street. Then the strangest coincidence. There on the corner of Earling Street and the Avenue was Frankie the Midget's big box-like Packard, parked by the curb. Frankie was sitting inside it behind the wheel, with a big cigar in his mouth, watching the people go by. Frankie had a special seat that propped him up high. Seraphin had never seen the inside of Frankie's Packard, but it must have been specially built for him. How else could he reach the gas pedal?

Doyle's place was close by. Seraphin decided to try Jimmy first. He felt more at ease with Jimmy than he did with Frankie. Jimmy was more happy-go-lucky. Frankie had a smoldering look to him, like he was bitter about something. No, it wasn't bitter. More sad.

You couldn't miss Doyle's place. Doyle's face looked at you from all the windows. In fact, the giant posters of his face completely covered the windows; you couldn't see inside the store. Doyle was not looking off into the distance. It was a front view. Each poster said on the top:

For Mayor

Then came his face. Then below his face:

John "Jack" Doyle
The People's Choice

87

The door was open. Seraphin peeked inside. The store was actually pretty empty. There was one big table with campaign stuff on top of it, cards, pictures of Doyle, stuff like that. There were a few chairs about, the kind that fold up, and that was about it. Jimmy was sitting in one of the chairs, which was really too small to hold his big bottom, and he glanced up at Seraphin.

Seraphin went in.

Jimmy was dressed differently than usual. It was the first time Seraphin had ever seen him in a suit and wearing a tie. But Seraphin noticed that Jimmy had loosened the tie and unbuttoned the top button of his shirt. Also the collar of his white shirt was frayed. It was not a new shirt.

On the wall was a giant sign. It said:

Doyle for Mayor
North End Campaign Headquarters

Seraphin held the nickel out to Jimmy. "This is from Joe the Cobbler." He said that even though Jimmy knew who he was. "He wants to play five-seven-three, boxed."

Jimmy took the nickel. Then he reached in a pocket, took out a little book, wrote something in it, and put the book back.

"Tell your father for me to vote for Doyle," Jimmy said.

"I will," Seraphin said, trying hard to suppress a smile. He knew how Pa felt about Irish politicians.

Jimmy had noticed him eyeing the stuff on the table when he walked in. He indicated the small cards. "You want a couple of these?"

Seraphin nodded.

"Help yourself."

Seraphin did, taking two.

"Thank you," Seraphin said.

"Here, I'm going to give you something. Give this to Joe."

Jimmy reached in the lapel pocket of his suit coat and brought out a calling card. He handed it to Seraphin, who read it. Jimmy watched his face while he read it. It said in the middle:

Doyle for Mayor

Then in the lower left-hand corner in smaller type it said:

James Gallagher
Assistant Campaign Manager
North End

"I'm the Assistant Campaign Manager for the whole North End," Jimmy said with pride.

"That's good, Jimmy. That's really good," Seraphin complimented him.

"You show that card to your father," Jimmy said. "I want him to see it. Because I like Joe. He's always been straight with me. A lot of people now, they come around me, since I was appointed, but I don't pay any attention to them. I don't care if I do end up someplace with this. I'll still remember Joe. Because he's straight."

"Okay, Jimmy, thank you. I'll take it to my father."

"Do you want a card for yourself?"

"Sure."

Jimmy brought out another calling card and handed it to Seraphin.

"Thanks, Jimmy."

Just then a drunk guy came in and walked with uncertain steps toward them. He needed a shave bad. But he was in a good mood, smiling broadly.

"Where's that deadbeat Doyle?" the drunk called in greeting. "Or should I say—His Honor the Mayor?"

"Let's have a little respect around here, Bronko," Jimmy said, but he was laughing when he said it.

Seraphin slipped out then.

Frankie the Midget looked at Seraphin with interest as he walked by, as if he knew why Seraphin had gone in there.

When Seraphin got back to the shop, Pa had just sat down on the stool by the sewing machine, starting his dinner.

Seraphin showed him Jimmy's calling card.

"He's the Assistant Campaign Manager for the whole North End." Seraphin said.

"Yes, I know," Pa said. "Jimmy told me. If Doyle wins, Jimmy will have a job with him. Jimmy will have an office in the City Hall. He will be in charge of meeting the public. If you have a complaint, you go see Jimmy. If the garbage man puts a dent in your garbage can, you go see Jimmy.

89

"This Jimmy is a bum. He never worked a day in his life. But if this Doyle wins, Jimmy will become an official in the government. He will have a car and smoke cigars. This is America. That's how they do things here.

"Yes, it is a success story. You wait long enough and you will see Jimmy's picture in the paper yet, shaking hands with the Governor. In this country all things are possible and the more unbelievable they are, the more possible they are. It's a crazy country."

Seraphin was sitting in the chair.

Pa wasn't ready for dessert yet but he looked in the little white bag and took out the strawberry turnover. Then he called Seraphin over and offered him the white bag.

"Here, Seraphin. Take this cake."

Good manners required that he refuse.

"No, Pa, I bought that for you. Ma wants you to have it."

"No. One is enough for me. Here."

"You're sure you don't want it?"

"I'm sure."

"Okay, Pa. Thank you."

He took the white bag. Looking inside it, he saw the lemon turnover. Aaahhhh.

CHAPTER 9

Secundo B. Alves

Seraphin was in the house when he heard the croak of the ragman coming through the open window.

"Rakes. Battle-akes."

What the ragman was really saying was, "Rags. Bottles-rags."

Seraphin dashed down the stairs after him.

"Hey! Hey, mister!"

The ragman turned on the top of his cart and saw Seraphin running after him. He pulled the horse over to the curb.

"Whatchagot?"

"I got some rags."

"How much you got?"

"I got a burlap bag filled with them."

The ragman grunted in reply and got down off the cart. The cart was filled with bundles of newspaper and bags of rags. The horse turned his head sideways and watched the ragman go with Seraphin.

Seraphin led the way toward the cellar door in the back yard. You had to go down the cellar stairs but the back piazza was built low over the stairs.

"Watch your head," he advised the ragman.

You had to bend way down or you would hit your head on the beam of the back piazza. And there was no use getting the guy mad at him. Once he brought a ragman down here and didn't bother telling him to duck. The guy conked his head on the beam and almost knocked himself out.

They made it safely into the cellar.

Seraphin brought out the rags.

The ragman put his hand inside the burlap bag and felt all around to make sure there was nothing inside but rags. Then he caught the bag with his hook, lifted it up in the air, and looked at the scale. Seraphin was leaning close, trying to see.

"Twelve pounds. Six cents," the ragman announced.

Seraphin was disappointed. He was hoping for more than that. He wanted to get a dime, enough to go to the show.

"Don't I get something for the bag?"

"The bag? Huh! Not worth nothing."

"They used to be worth a cent."

"Huh! Not no more. Not worth nothing today."

The ragman looked around the cellar. This made Seraphin uneasy. He didn't want the ragman stealing any of Pa's things, which were all over the cellar.

"Got anything else?"

Seraphin shook his head.

"Paper?"

"No."

Wait! Yes! Bottles! He had gone to the Dump a long time ago with his team and salvaged a whole bunch of bottles. They were in a cardboard box in a dark far corner of the cellar. Shuffling along sort of sideways, so as to keep an eye on the ragman, Seraphin went for the box of bottles.

He placed the box in front of the ragman. There were eight bottles. None of them were soda bottles of course, for those he could sell to the stores. There were two brown beer bottles, one small maple syrup bottle with a handle on it, one long skinny vinegar bottle, one bleach bottle, one quart pickle jar, one bottle he didn't know what it was used for, and then the one he had the highest hopes for—a big gallon wine jug.

The ragman looked at them. He shook his head. "No good."

Seraphin had been hoping to get a cent each, and maybe as much as a nickel for the gallon jug.

"No good to me."

"How much you give me for all of them?"

"I'll give you a cent for the whole business," the ragman said with a weary indifference.

"Okay, I'll take it."

That made seven cents. The ragman brought out a pouch filled with coins. He poured some of the coins into his hand and picked out seven coppers. He handed them to Seraphin without a word.

Seraphin helped the ragman carry the stuff out. Seraphin took the box of bottles and the ragman carried the rags. The ragman threw the bag of rags up on the cart. The bottles he placed carefully up in the front of the cart under his seat. He smashed the box with his feet and put the flattened cardboard under a bag of rags.

Seraphin watched him go off. Fred Farnsworth had told Pa about a ragman in Shefford. The ragman had died and they found fifteen thousand dollars in cash sewed up inside his mattress. Pa marveled at the story, that a man could save up that much from just buying rags from kids. Seraphin wondered about this ragman. Did he have fifteen thousand dollars sewed up inside his mattress?

Just then Chimp Silva came out of his house. He was walking purposefully down the street. Chimp was always going someplace.

"Whattaya doin', Seraphin?"

"Nothing."

"You wanna have some fun?"

"Yeah."

"Come on with me then."

"Where are you going?"

"To a rally for Secundo B. Alves. He's running for Mayor."

This was the first he had heard that Secundo B. Alves was running for Mayor. He had heard Pa mention him a couple of times. Secundo B. Alves was a Portuguese lawyer with an office in the North End. Seraphin didn't know any more about him than that.

Seraphin marched side by side with Chimp.

"Where's it going to be?"

"You know where the Ponta Delgada Club is on North Bridge Street?"

"Yeah. I know where it is."

"Well, right inside the club."

Usually you couldn't see inside the Ponta Delgada Social Club. It was right on the corner of Bullock and North Bridge. It used to be a store, but they had gone and painted all the windows, including the glass on the door, dark green. So you couldn't see inside. But sometimes in the summertime they let the door stay open to get a little breeze, and then you could see inside when you walked by.

Seraphin always stared inside when he walked by. He was curious about this club, what they did inside. Mostly he saw the men sitting around card tables, playing cards, while smoking cigarettes and drinking from small bottles of soda. He saw the corner of the pool table and heard the clicking of the balls. And occasionally he heard an unseen singer, strumming the Portuguese guitar, and singing some sad lines in a voice filled with feeling.

When Chimp and Seraphin got to the club, the sidewalk and the doorway were crowded with men, standing around, talking. Chimp slipped through the crowd. Seraphin followed him.

The door was wide open but a barrel-chested man stood in the doorway, facing out. Seraphin could see behind him rows of chairs, with many already occupied.

"Where do you think you're going?" the big man asked Chimp sternly. "No kids allowed."

"My father's in there," Chimp said. "Me and my brother have got to see him."

"What's your father's name?"

"*Senhor* Fonseca," Chimp lied easily. Seraphin had to marvel at Chimp, not just his nerve, but his quick thinking. He was so smooth, he hadn't searched his mind for a name and given it away by hesitating. *Senhor* Fonseca, just like that, quick and easy, just like it was his own name.

The man looked at Chimp, frowning.

"It won't take a minute," Chimp said, looking him in the eye.

"Okay," the man said.

Once inside, Chimp murmured in Seraphin's ear. "Let's split up so we won't attract attention. Sit by somebody and talk to him. Everybody'll think you're with the guy and they won't bother you."

Seraphin was thinking fast. If accosted, he had to have a story ready. He had been told by his mother to meet his father here and give him a message. He was waiting for his father now. That would do it. If he told them that, they wouldn't dare throw him out. Or would they?

Seraphin saw an old man with pink cheeks and a snowy white mane talking animatedly to a younger man seated beside him. The old man looked very clean and he sat erect. Seraphin sat down next to him.

The old man slapped a newspaper. "Look at this! Divorced for the fourth time! Whore! Prostitute! She should sell herself in the streets!" And he looked fiercely at Seraphin. His eyes were bright blue. Seraphin marveled, for he had never before seen a Portuguese with blue eyes.

The younger man was smiling. "Don't get so excited, *Senhor* Rezendes. It's not good for the digestion."

"Did you hear Father Cordeiro in church on Sunday? The lovers now come into his yard at night and make love right under his window. In his own yard! Is that not an outrage?"

"What do you expect? His yard has the only piece of grass in the whole of North Bridge Street. Where else can lovers go? Tell him to trample all the lovely flowers in his garden. Tell him to chop down that shade tree in the middle of his lawn. Tell him to knock down the high fence that keeps his yard a rare jewel. And then tell him to cover the whole thing with cement. He will not be bothered by lovers any more. Instead of complaining, he should rejoice that he has such a paradise of a yard and he should be willing to share it."

"That's it, Adelino. Make fun of the priest. Make jokes. Laugh. But Someone is listening to you. He is taking note of what you say."

"And what is he doing up at two in the morning? Why isn't he asleep like a good priest?"

"They wake him with their noises! With their animal noises!"

The younger man laughed. "You have forgotten, old man. When you're young, the juices flow."

The old man sat quietly morose for a moment. "I see them in the church," he said quietly. "The boys and girls sitting there with an expression of reverence on their faces. But I see their hands passing notes back and forth. Don't you think I see that? I see them making their dates under the priest's nose. During Mass! During Mass! When their thoughts should be on God!"

And he looked accusingly at Seraphin.

"You take things to heart too much, *Senhor* Rezendes. Doesn't your faith give you any peace?"

"Adelino, you don't fool me. You are a good Catholic. I know that. And I'm going to tell you something. Think of this now. I keep having this dream. If in a year's time I went out and got one person to join the Catholic Church, and you went out and got another person to join the

95

Catholic Church, and if all the other Catholics did the same thing, each convincing one person of the beauty and the eternal truth of our faith, and then the next year all the Catholics did the same thing again, and then the third year the same thing, and so on—why, in five years' time the whole world would be Catholic."

"And I'd still be working only two days a week."

"You think only of your stomach! And looking at the women! The animal passions!"

"And when you were my age, were you any different?"

"But I am wiser now."

"And when I reach your age, God willing—I will be wiser, too."

Seraphin looked around at the club. It was really starting to get packed. There were no women present. It was all men.

The old man turned to Seraphin. "Are you voting this year?" he asked, straight-faced.

"No, not this year," Seraphin said with a smile.

"Do you go to church?"

"Yes." Once in a while, Seraphin amended to himself.

"Good."

"Are you hungry?"

"No."

"How about a nice doughnut?"

"Well. . . ."

"Here, I'll get you one."

The old man got up and went over to the side. There was a table there with food on it. To Seraphin's amazement he saw Chimp there, helping himself. What guts Chimp had. Seraphin then quickly looked away because he didn't want the old man to think he was watching him bringing him back food. That would have been bad manners.

"His bark is worse than his bite," the younger man said to Seraphin in explanation.

The old man returned with two doughnuts and a paper cup. He handed Seraphin both doughnuts. "I brought you my share, too." And then he handed him the paper cup. "This will help wash them down." The paper cup was filled with coffee. "I put milk and sugar in it for you. You don't drink it straight, do you?"

"No. Thank you very much."

Seraphin took a bite of the first doughnut. It was delicious. He looked at the coffee. It was the first time in his life he had ever had coffee. They drank only tea at his house. Of course, he and Laura drank milk mostly. But Ma loved tea and she drank a lot of it, and on cold winter nights she always gave Pa a cup of hot tea with his meal when he came home from work. But never coffee.

He took a sip of it. He tried not to make a face. It wasn't like tea at all. It wasn't sweet at all. It was strong and almost bitter. Because the old man had gotten it for him, he would have to drink it all. But he wasn't looking forward to it.

There was a commotion behind them. A group of excited men was slowly making its way into the club. In the center of the group, surrounded and escorted, was a man Seraphin assumed to be Secundo B. Alves. He had never seen him before. The group made its way to the small raised platform at the front. There the President of the Ponta Delgada Social Club got up on the platform and began introducing Secundo B. Alves. Seraphin stared at Secundo B. Alves.

He was a striking man. He was small and looked undernourished. His hair was black and coarse. It grew luxuriantly, wild and unmanageable, no part possible. He had the prominent Arab nose some Portuguese had. He had a wet mouth; his lower lip, which was quite fat, glistened. In repose, his lips curled and twisted in a vinegary pout. But then in an instant his face would be transformed and he would give a brilliant, flashing smile. But what held you was his eyes. They looked out at you with burning intensity. They held you in their penetrating, hypnotic gaze. Seraphin was glad he was sitting next to the old man for protection.

Then, his introduction finished, the President of the club stepped off the platform and Secundo B. Alves got on it. Everybody gave him a big hand. He acknowledged their applause with a slight bow.

"Oh, my countrymen!" he said. "How good it is to be here among you, to look out and see your honest Portuguese faces. This is where I belong. This is where I feel at home. Humble workers living a simple life, those are the Portuguese I know and love. No fine suits here. No expensive shoes. No 'big shots' here. The last place I spoke was in the banquet room of a fine restaurant. My audience was an association of American businessmen. But I did not feel at home with them. I feel more at home with you here in this modest club.

"And what a privilege to address you in the beautiful Portuguese language, the sweet Portuguese language that I love so, the language that is not words to me but music, so harmonious, so melodic, so expressive, so rich, so subtle, so powerful, so passionate! It is a language fit for a poet!"

He was holding a paper with writing on it, and he now began to wave the paper. "When I am among the Portuguese, I do not need notes!" he cried. "Let those who need a prepared speech use them!" And so saying, he crumpled the paper into a ball and hurled it to the floor. "I do not need notes! I will speak from here!" he exclaimed, thumping his heart four or five times. "And the Portuguese will hear me!" There was strong, spontaneous applause.

"I will confess to you. I can speak English just so long and then I have to speak Portuguese. And if there is no one around to speak it to, then I talk out loud to myself.

"English is a language without heart, without feeling. In English they call a woman who does not marry 'an old maid.' And they use this term in the most cruel, mocking way. It is a term of humiliation, of derision even. I met a very attractive woman of forty-five—I am not married yet so I am allowed to look—and an American said to me with the most possible contempt in his voice—'Oh, she's an old maid.' And they will even call a young woman of thirty that. So not only is it undignified, it is also illogical and inaccurate, for she is certainly not old.

"Now in Portuguese what do we call a woman who does not marry? We can her *uma solteira*. It means 'a woman living alone.' We use it as a term of sympathy. She is alone, she has no one to take care of her. And notice how logical it is. Married—together. Not married—alone. What could be more logical, more descriptive, more kind? You see the beauty of the Portuguese language? The superiority of the Portuguese language?

"I am running for the office of Mayor of Gaw. I am here to ask you for your vote. You know that. But why am I running for Mayor? What prompted me to get into politics? I am running because of something that happened just a few months ago. You may have read about it in the Portuguese paper. The *Evening Herald* didn't think it was important enough to put in their paper. You may have read that I was involved in a disturbance at a meeting of the Portuguese-American Civic Improvement League. But they didn't tell you the whole story. They didn't tell you I was thrown out. They didn't tell you I got my coat ripped. They told you I was asked to leave. That's not true. I was thrown out! Five or six big strong men grabbed me and pushed me out the door. And ripped my coat besides. The paper didn't tell you that I got my coat ripped. And the paper didn't tell you that the next day the police visited me and told me I must never go again to a meeting of the Portuguese-American Civic Improvement League or I would be arrested. That was when I decided to run for Mayor.

"Maybe you haven't heard very much about the Portuguese-American Civic Improvement League. I know I didn't know very much about them until I attended that meeting. It's a club of both men and women. And I tell you, there are no pool tables there!" There was much laughter at this. "The President of the club is a woman, the wife of Doctor Paiva, and I don't mean anything against Doctor Paiva by this, he is a fine doctor. But this club, what they do, is this. They charter a bus, and they go to Boston, and they spend the day walking around an art museum looking at the paintings, and then they stop at an elegant restaurant for a fine meal, and then when their bellies are full, they come back home, and that's how they improve the life of the Portuguese people in Gaw!

"But I was at their meeting and I sat there for about an hour, until I could stand no more, and what I heard in that hour was about two thousand committee reports. They had a committee to open the windows and another committee to close them. In this they follow the custom of the Americans. The Americans love committees.

"But finally I stood up and I said, 'It is now nine o'clock and I have been here since eight o'clock. I have been listening to you. I have heard 'Madame Chairman this' and 'Madame Chairman that' and I have heard 'Mr.' Souza, not *Senhor* Souza, and 'Mrs.' Almeida, not *Senhora* Almeida, and in all this time I have not heard a single word in Portuguese. I am thinking—When is somebody going to say something in Portuguese?

"And Doctor Paiva's wife at the head table, she had this big hammer made out of wood, and she looked at me and she said, 'We speak English here.'

"And I put my hand over my heart, like this, and I said, 'And I speak Portuguese here!'

"She said, 'It is in our Constitution.'

99

"And I said, 'To hell with your Constitution!'

"She started hitting the top of the table with that hammer. 'You are out of order!'

"And I said, 'No, it is you who is out of order! What is it? Do you want to be Americans so badly that you are ashamed to speak Portuguese? Have you forgotten the mother who gave birth to you? Have you forgotten your father's songs? Have you cast aside your heritage like a shameful thing? Call yourselves Portuguese? The next thing you will do is change your names!'

"Doctor Paiva's wife began hitting the table some more with her hammer.

"'You want to speak English here?' I said. 'All right! That's fine with me. I have no objection. But don't call yourselves the Portuguese-American Civic Improvement League! Leave the Portuguese out of it! Call yourselves the American Civic Improvement League! I see nothing Portuguese here!'

"Doctor Paiva's wife was hitting the table with the hammer and calling out, 'Sergeant-at-arms!' And I heard several voices in the audience yelling, 'Throw him out!'

"And then I noticed the two flags flying up in the front, the American flag and the Portuguese flag, and I ran to them and I shouted. 'It's a sacrilege to fly the Portuguese flag in this place! How can you do it? Hypocrites!' And I started to take the Portuguese flag down and that was when the men grabbed me and dragged me to the door and threw me out.

"Well, I'm sure I lost some votes over there."

"But you'll get them back here, Secundo!" a voice called out with feeling.

There was strong applause.

"They are not the true Portuguese over there in the Portuguese-American Civic Improvement League. They may be wearing the nice clothes. They may be wearing the suit and tie. They may have a car. They may live in the nice houses. But they are not the true Portuguese. The true Portuguese are here before me in this club.

"And that's why I am asking for your vote. I want to be the voice of the true Portuguese people. I want to be the voice of your aspirations, your dreams.

"The Portuguese are the unknown people. We are lost in this vast country. Nobody knows we are here. To be Portuguese in America is to be a stone dropped in the middle of the ocean. It sinks beneath the waves and vanishes without a trace.

"We are to be swallowed up in America. That is our destiny. But before that happens, I want to make the greatness of the Portuguese soul, the spirituality of the Portuguese people known to all America! That is why I ask you to vote for me! The Portuguese people must have some influence in this country. There are no Portuguese judges in America, no representatives, no mayors. We work hard. We never complain. We die quietly. We must now speak!

"The Italian people have influence in America. Did you ever look at the history book your children bring home from school? It's all about Columbus. Columbus proved the world was round, the book says. Columbus proved no such thing! All Columbus did was take a short trip. How do you prove the world is round? You start at one place and sail all the way around the world and end up at that same place—that's the only way to prove the world is round, and Magellan did that! But because Columbus was Italian and Magellan was Portuguese, your child's history book has everything about Columbus, cracking an egg and Queen Isabella selling her jewels and all that stuff, but nothing about Magellan. And we celebrate Columbus Day. By rights, it should be Magellan Day!

"Yes, the Italian people have influence in America. That is because there are Italian judges, Italian representatives, and Italian mayors. They are spokesmen for the Italian point of view. And that is what the Portuguese people must do. We must elect some Portuguese to office.

"Look at what happened in Providence the other day. An Italian gangster was shot dead in the street. He was going into a big department store. Three other Italians stepped out of a car, walked over to him, and shot him dead right there on the sidewalk. Now listen to this. The three Italians who shot him were so bold and unafraid that the witnesses said they walked slowly back to their car. That's how safe they felt. They did not run back to their car, they walked slowly back, very calm, and drove away. And they shot this man in broad daylight in front of fifteen witnesses. And the police say they cannot find the killers. They have no clues.

"Do you know why this is so, why the police cannot find those killers? Because in this country the Italians have influence. In this country when a prominent Italian gangster dies, the Mayor and the Chief of Police attend his funeral.

"But let a Portuguese steal fifty cents in the middle of the night. Let him wear a mask so that no one will recognize him. Let him wear gloves so as not to leave fingerprints. Let him get on a bus the next morning and run away to Kansas to try to hide there. No. No luck. The police will find him quickly and bring him back. And do you know why this is so? Because the Portuguese people have no influence! And when you have no influence, the whole world is looking and watching for you and they will drop the whole load on you.

"Nobody in America knows the greatness of the Portuguese people. They do not know our glorious history. Even our own children do not know our history. The history books in the schools here are all written by Protestants! They won't give Catholics credit for anything! But we were the most powerful nation on earth! Our intrepid sailors voyaged to the far corners of the globe! The riches of the world were ours! The silks, the spices, the rare jewels, they were all ours! The East Indies were ours! India was ours! Then the robbers came! The Dutch, the English, the French, they stole everything from us!"

Foam was bubbling in the corners of Secundo B. Alves's mouth.

"Do you know the Japanese did not have the word 'thank you' in their vocabulary? We taught them how to say it. *Obrigado*! But they could not pronounce it right. In their mouths it came out *Arigato*. And that's how they say it today, *Arigato*. But they learned the word from us—they learned to say thank you in gratitude to the people who brought them the light of Jesus. The Americans always brag they are first in everything. They brag about Admiral Perry going to Japan. We were in Japan two hundred years before the Declaration of Independence!

"Tell your sons never to forget that they are Portuguese! Tell them of Da Gama! What a great name! What a great man!

"I see a ship plowing bravely through the unknown sea, a sea full of peril and danger. And in the dark of night comes a violent storm. The sea is running wild. The waves are mountainous. The wind is shrieking. The proud mast sways before the fury of the wind. The ship groans in the ferocity of the storm's attack. And on the storm-drenched deck I see Da Gama at the helm. His grasp is firm. And when so many on the voyage have lost hope, I hear his calm voice—'Do not despair, my countrymen. I shall take you to a safe harbor.'

"The spirit of Da Gama lives in each of you, my dear friends. He sailed off into the unknown. So did you. He sailed through storms. So did you. He suffered privations. So did you. He was a man of great courage. So are you. You left everything behind. Your homes. Your loved ones. Your language. Your culture. Everything that meant life to you! And you forsook it all for this wilderness of America—to provide bread for the mouths of your children. To your sons, tell them—'Never forget! You are Portuguese! Be proud of it!'

"And so we took ourselves away from the land of our birth, away from the land of our fathers. We find ourselves in America. But, my dear friends, is it not true that in the early evening you can still hear the village church bell calling you to prayer? *Booong!*" He made the sound deep in his throat. *"Booong! Booong! Booong!* Nothing can compare with that peace. No money or material wealth of any kind can buy it. Therefore we are more than rich men. We have our foundation firm and nothing can move it or destroy it. Our mothers and fathers in their faith had all that God gave them in this world, faith in Him, and in the next world the joy of seeing Him in all his splendor!

"I was walking in the Brookhaven Cemetery last year and I saw a hearse race in, the young driver and his helper jump out, they take out the coffin, laughing and joking all the while, set it down on the ground there, by an open grave, and jump back in their hearse and race out. And I thought, 'My God! The poor creature has no mourners!' Is it possible that in America you can die alone like an old dog in the corner, with your face to the wall? Will they race you to the cemetery and bury you hurriedly and without feeling, like a loathsome thing?

"I remember *Tia Maria* in my village on Saint Michael. She was no one's aunt but everybody called her that. She was an old lady, poor, very poor. She existed on the bounty of others. When we made something, some little dish, our mothers would say, 'Here. This portion is for *Tia Maria*. Take it to her.' And when she died—" his voice choked, his eyes watered, and he drew the wet noisily back up his nose "—and when she died, her coffin was carried on foot through the streets from the church to the graveyard, and the whole village walked behind the coffin, every-

103

body, the mothers, the fathers, the children, everybody crying, the whole village accompanying her to her last resting place, everybody there to give homage and respect and love to the departed one, everybody crying for their beloved *Tia Maria,* and I think of that coffin sitting on the ground in the Brookhaven Cemetery all by itself. . . ."

And now the tears ran openly down his cheeks, unstoppable.

He put his hands up by his shoulders, palms open to the audience, in the surrender position, and kept shaking his head sideways, meaning, "I cannot go on. I cannot continue."

The club erupted. The applause was like an explosion. From all over there came emotional cries, ringing cries of feeling, shouts of approbation. Everybody was on his feet. The old man next to Seraphin was crying, as were many others. There was a surge toward Secundo B. Alves. Everybody wanted to be near him.

Seraphin had never heard a speaker like him before. He had been in complete control of his audience. They had been silent, attentive, hanging on his every word.

Seraphin knew one thing. Secundo B. Alves was going to win the election. He was such a great speaker he couldn't lose. Everybody was going to vote for him.

CHAPTER 10

Teddy's Daughter

Pa came home for supper at his usual time, almost ten o'clock. He put the dinner bag down on the floor, washed his hands, and immediately sat down at the table. He tore off a chunk of Portuguese bread and started eating while he waited for Ma to heat the soup. Sometimes Pa would eat half a loaf while he waited.

Except for the bread, Ma's soup would be the whole meal. Of course, Ma's soups were not like American soups. Once Seraphin had had Campbell's Tomato Soup and he didn't like it at all. First, the chemicals in it burned his throat. Second, it was all liquid. Ma's soups were rich with meat and vegetables. Her soups filled you up. And they didn't burn your throat with chemicals either.

Whatever amount of soup was left in the pot, Pa always finished it off, seconds, thirds, fourths, he didn't care. Ma just kept refilling his plate until the pot was empty.

Tonight it was kale soup, with big pieces of linguiça in it. Ma, Laura, and Seraphin had eaten a lot earlier, at six o'clock. Of course, what Ma usually did, to save the soup for Pa, she would give them just a little taste of it and give them something else instead, like a pork chop or hamburger with mashed potatoes. Also, to tell the truth, Ma did that because Seraphin and Laura got tired of eating just soup. Pa never did, however.

After a few minutes a plate of hot kale soup was in front of Pa. In between and during mouthfuls, Pa started talking about things, as he always did.

"Today," he said, "I spoke with Teddy. You know Teddy?" he said, looking at Ma.

Ma had never met Teddy but she had heard about him from Pa.

"Yes," Ma said, "the one who runs the bakery."

"Yes. Yes. Exactly," Pa said. "He has a good business. A very good business. The Polockas are like the Portuguese. Each people likes its own bread, and Teddy has the only Polocka bakery in the North End. All the bread eaten by the Polockas is baked by him. But anyway I like Teddy. He works very hard, like I do. And he is an honest man, a serious man.

"I was there working in the shop when I looked out the window and I saw Teddy's bread truck drive up and park at the curb there. The whole truck was covered with big signs—*Vote for Grabowski*—on the side, on the back, even on top of the truck they had put kind of like a billboard. Then this man got out of the truck and he was dressed in funny clothes, but when I saw his face, I saw it was Teddy. He was wearing a shirt that had lots of lace on it, crazy-looking pants that came only to his knees, white stockings that went all the way up to his pants, and shoes that looked like ladies' shoes.

"I went out in the doorway and I called to him.

"'Hey, Teddy!' I said. 'Come over here! I want to talk to you.'

"He came to my shop and he entered inside. Poor man, he looked very unhappy, very embarrassed, you know.

"'Teddy,' I said, 'why are you dressed like a clown?'

"'Joe,' he said, 'I'm working for Lawyer Grabowski.'

"'Teddy,' I said, 'you an honest man. You work for your living. Why you want to mix up with those people for?'

"'I'm trying to help Grabowski make a good showing,' he said.

"'And you're helping him by going around dressed like a clown?' I said.

"'I go with Grabowski to the clubs,' he said 'We just got back from the Polish-American War Veterans Club. I'm supposed to be Count Pulaski. He's some fellow that fought for this country. I go up in the front and Grabowski's son comes with me. He's dressed like George Washington. And I say some lines and he says some lines, and then we sit down and Grabowski gets up and makes a speech.'

"'I thought you were a baker, Teddy,' I said. 'I didn't know you were an actor.'

"'I have to do this, Joe,' he said. 'I'm doing it for my daughter. I sent her to college to be teacher and she graduate. But she can't get no teaching job here. The School Board gives the jobs to their friends. So now she's stitching shirts in the sweatshop. It's the only job she can get. Every day I see her, looking so sad. It breaks my heart. So I said to myself, "I have to try to do something for her."'"

Seraphin knew who his daughter was. She had been pointed out to him by Pa. She walked by Pa's shop every day, going to and from work. She walked with her eyes on the ground. She never looked up. She really did look sad.

"'So I went to see Lawyer Grabowski,' Teddy said. 'I told him about my daughter, and I said, "What can I do to help her?"

"'And Grabowski said to me, "Teddy, if you work for me in this election and I make a good showing, then maybe I can do something for her. You see, the School Board members are going to come up for re-election, and they're going to want my support. They're going to want me to endorse them. So if I do that for them, then they're going to be willing to do a favor for me. I'll tell them to put your daughter's name on the list for teacher."

"'So, Joe, I had no choice. If you could see my girl's face at the table, every night, night after night, you'd do the same thing. She never complains. But I can see her going down, less and less talk, less and less smiles. I've got to do this, Joe!'"

Pa stopped talking then and concentrated on eating, while everybody was thinking about the story Pa had just told them.

"Pa, who do you think is going to win the election?" Seraphin suddenly asked.

Pa, his eyes bright with interest, looked at Seraphin.

"Why, who do you think is going to win?"

"I think Secundo B. Alves is going to win."

Pa burst out with a merry laugh.

"Seraphin," he said, shaking his head, "don't you know that Secundo B. Alves has no chances? None. No chances at all. What makes you think he is going to win?"

"I heard him make a speech at the Ponta Delgada Club. Everybody cheered him when he finished."

"Sure," Pa said, "everybody cheered. But who was there? All Portuguese, huh? You see, Seraphin, all the Portuguese will vote for Secundo B. Alves, but there are not enough Portuguese in the city to elect him. Just like Grabowski with the Polockas. The Polockas vote for him but there's not enough Polockas to make a majority. Same thing with that Langevin and the French. They will all lose."

Seraphin was dumbfounded. Was it really so? He had never thought of it that way before. Was each man's nationality his strength and ultimately his weakness also? Yes, it must be so. Logic would say that it was so.

Seraphin pursued the subject. "Does Secundo B. Alves know he is going to lose?"

"Sure he knows. He is no fool."

"Then why is he running?"

"'Why is he running?'" Pa repeated. "He is running because he wants to make the free advertise. You see, Seraphin, in this city there are maybe fifty lawyers, but there is only work for maybe five of them. The lawyers who are quiet, nobody ever hears of them, they get no business. But the lawyer with the big mouth, everybody hears of him. You see his name in the paper. You hear his name on the radio. Then when you get into some trouble with the law, you need a lawyer. Who do you think of going to? You think of going to this man you have heard about, naturally. And that is what Alves is trying to do. He's trying to advertise his name so that when a Portuguese is in trouble, he will come to Secundo B. Alves. And that's why he's running for Mayor. To drum up some business. He goes to all the Portuguese clubs and appeals to all the simple-minded souls there."

"Listen to who's calling the Portuguese simple-minded!" Ma said.

"Yes, they are simple-minded," Pa said. "Because they are living in America and they think they can live the same way they did back in Portugal. It can't be! This is a new country with new ways. If you want to live with the old ways, then you should to stay in Portugal. Only a fool would come to a new country and expect to live the same way he lived in the old country. This Alves he goes around telling people he misses the religious processions of his village on St. Michael. Jesus comes walking down the street with His cross and all the people throw flowers on the street where He walks. The whole street loaded with flowers from end to end. And he's mad because nobody in America throws flowers on the street. If you want to throw flowers on the street, then stay on St. Michael. Don't come here."

"You can say that because you are a man without religion," Ma said.

"But that is what Secundo B. Alves is trying to do. Make some business. Up to now he has barely been able to pay his rent. He sits there in his office, killing flies."

"Killing flies" was Pa's favorite phrase to show his derisive judgment of a business failure. It meant that the individual had no customers, nothing to do, so in his boredom he passed the time away in his office or store by killing flies.

"So I take it you're not going to vote for Secundo B. Alves," Ma said.

"No, I'm not," Pa said. "I wouldn't vote for that windbag," and Pa opened and closed his mouth rapidly and repeatedly, saying, *"Blah-blah-blah-blah,"* and with his hands cutting the air sharply with the emphatic gesticulations of the orator.

Actually, Secundo B. Alves did not speak that way, as Seraphin remembered.

109

"What do you think about Doyle?" Seraphin asked. "Do you think he has a chance?"

"I think he has a chance, but I'm not going to vote for him. I would sooner vote for the devil. The Irish are good for two things—drinking and stealing. They lived that way in Ireland, stealing from each other, so when they came to this country, they kept it up, the old ways of stealing everything they can. I don't want to give that man the license to put his hand in my pocket."

"Nobody pleases you," Ma said. "Everybody has something wrong with him. Tell me, O Wise One, who are you going to vote for?"

"For my part, I like Mayor Mayhew," Pa said. "His father started the Mayhew Mill. It takes a lot of brains to run a big mill like that, hundreds of employees."

"That was the father," Ma said. "Maybe the son doesn't have the father's brains."

"Mayor Mayhew has a good education," Pa went on smoothly.

"What about Secundo B. Alves and Grabowski?" Ma reminded him. "They are both lawyers. Didn't they have to go to college and get an education, too?"

"They are lawyers but they are penniless lawyers!" Pa exclaimed, stung. "They are beggars! The beggar selling pencils in front of the Five and Ten Cent Store, the one with no legs and sitting on a cart, he has as much money as they do!"

"You judge a man by how much money he has!" Ma charged fiercely.

"I'm going to explain this to you," Pa said to Ma. "And listen carefully, I want you to understand this. Whenever you see a poor man running for Mayor, watch out. Suppose he wins. He will only be in office two years. Then he might lose. So that doesn't give him much time. Two years. He was poor before this and he will be poor after this. So this is his big chance. The big chance of his life. To enrich himself. He must steal and steal fast.

"Of all the candidates," Pa went on, "Mayor Mayhew is the only rich man. Mayor Mayhew doesn't have to steal. He has plenty of money. He lives in a big house. That is why I think this city is safest in his hands. You understand? He didn't come to fill his pockets."

"You think everybody is a crook," Ma said.

"If you put meat before the wolf, he will eat it. And these politicians are mostly all wolves. Do you think they go up and down the city exercising their lungs, braying at the moon, just for the hell of it? They expect to get paid."

They all sat quietly for a time. Then Pa got his good humor back.

"One thing I am going to do," he said with a laugh, "I am going to play a trick on Lawyer Grabowski. Yes, I am going to play a trick on that guy. You know, he is very strong in Heap Square, because of all the Polockas that live there in the surrounding streets. So one of his men came to see me, not Teddy, and this fellow come in the shop, introduce himself, told me he is working for Grabowski, and he said to me, 'We want your vote.'

"I said to him—'You got my vote!'

"And he said to me—'You going to vote for Grabowski?'

"And I said to him—'Yes, I am going to vote for Grabowski!'

"'Good!' he said. 'Now if we can do anything for you, drive you to the polls, anything like that, you tell me, and we'll make arrangements.'

"Well, I think fast, right then and there. Here was an opportunity. When I vote, I have to close the shop early. It costs me a lot of work time. Because the fire station is so far away. It's the fire station by this house, not the one by my shop. But if I could have a ride, I could be there in a few minutes.

"So I got smart right there. I told him, 'Yes, I need a ride. Otherwise I'm not sure I will vote.'

"He took the bait.

"'That's no trouble,' he said. 'I will send a car around for you—you tell me what time you want to go—and we will pick you up, take you to the polls, wait for you, and then bring you back here to your shop.'

"'Okay. Good,' I said. Not only take me there but bring me back, too! This was a good piece of luck! So we made the appointment. In the morning when business is slow anyway, they're going to pick me up. And I will vote without walking a step. It will be done so fast I will not even notice it.

"So, thank you, Lawyer Grabowski," Pa said, "you help me a lot. But I will vote for Mayhew."

"That's a dirty trick," Laura said, disapproving. "You're accepting that ride under false pretenses, Pa. That's not right."

"He likes to play dirty tricks," Ma said, "but let somebody play one on him. Then it's a different story."

Pa's answer was to laugh in pure enjoyment.

111

CHAPTER 11

AT THE THEATRE

It was one o'clock Sunday afternoon. They had just finished dinner, but   *113*
they were still at the table.

Pa and Laura were having an argument over what show Laura
should go to. Laura was planning on going to the Royale Theatre,
which was just three blocks from their house, on the Avenue. Pa
wanted her to go to the Globe Theatre, which was in Heap Square,
across the street from his shop. The Royale was fifteen cents, and the
Globe was ten cents. That extra five cents was what bothered Pa, even
though it was her own money she was spending. It was just the princi-
ple of the thing.

"You got money to throw away, Laura?" Pa said. "The Globe shows
the same pictures."

"Sure, in about six months," Laura said.

"You can't wait six months? Is the picture a piece of fruit? Is it going
to spoil and get rotten in six months?"

"Pa, I would be the laughingstock at the store if it ever got out that
I went to the Globe. You know what everybody calls that place? The
Bughouse."

"There's no bugs there no more," Pa said. "There used to be in the
old days, yes. People caught lice there from one another, sitting so close
together, you know. But nobody has caught any bugs for many years.
They use powerful chemicals there, fumigate the whole show. I can
smell the smell from my shop. The chemicals kill all the bugs. No bugs
can live with those chemicals, I tell you."

"Well, you remember that time you and me went to the Globe,
Ma?" Laura said. "All through the picture I kept feeling like something

was biting me. Sharp bites. When I got home, I couldn't find any bite marks on me. But even if it was just my imagination, it spoiled the picture for me. I'm never going there again."

"Oh, man, let her go where she wants to go," Ma said. "Not everybody's a tightwad like you."

"Well, I don't want to take any chances," Laura said. "Not for five cents I don't. Besides, all the cheap people go there, Pa. All those Polocks from Heap Square. And the Portagees from North Bridge Street, the greenhorns from the old country."

"They bother you? They interfere with your watching the picture?"

"Yes, they bother me! That time with Ma this pig, this big dumb Polock, let a fart just as loud as you please, and everybody started laughing. They acted like it was a joke. I was so embarrassed."

"All right," Pa said, surrendering. "Don't go to the Globe. You are shocked by one fart. But I tell you what I am going to do. I am going to the Royale, too. Yes, today, I will go. And I will sit directly behind you. And I will let such a big fart I will dirty my pants. Then we will see if you will ever go to the Royale again."

"You'd never do it, Pa," Laura said. "You'd never pay the fifteen cents to get in."

"This once I would!" he vowed. "It would be worth it."

Actually, Laura hadn't told Pa about the group at the Globe that bothered her the most. They were the old poor. They were the same people who came to the fruit store and bought from the back. At the fruit store the choice and more expensive fruit was up front. As you went toward the back of the store, the quality and the prices of the fruit dropped. And the old poor never even looked at the front. They always waited patiently for her at the back to buy one tomato, two potatoes. Their pitiful purchases came out to three cents, five cents, never more than ten cents. And these old people in their shabby, threadbare clothes she saw again in the Globe. All the misery in the world was reflected in their faces—apologetic, pathetic, abject, hopeless, beaten-down faces. She didn't want to be around these old people. How could she enjoy a picture sitting next to one of them? When she was watching a gay romance, when she was dancing with the hero, swirling down the floor, in a lovely waltz, dancing with the Emperor in Old Vienna, and she'd hear one of the old poor cough with that racking cough, why, that cough would take her forcibly right out of that ballroom, right out of that castle, and take her right back to picking out one tomato in the back of the Old Colony Fruit Store in Gaw. She didn't want anybody or anything around her to remind her of the fruit store.

The Royale was the theatre for her. The extra five cents kept the cheap people out. And they didn't show cowboy pictures or horror films or serials. That kept the little kids away. They showed good pictures made by the big studios with stars you knew. They didn't show pictures by studios like Republic or Monogram, both of which made the most terrible, junky pictures. Of course, she could have gone to the Bijou Theatre downtown. The Bijou got good pictures and showed them a couple of months before the Royale. It cost a lot more. The Bijou was twenty-five cents on Sunday, and then there were two tokens for the streetcar, seven cents each way, making it thirty-nine cents in all. The couple of times she went, Pa had a fit about it, because it cost four times more than the Globe. But she didn't like to go to the Bijou and she never went there any more. It wasn't the money. And it wasn't the inconvenience and the bother, all that time wasted standing around waiting for a streetcar. It was just that she didn't feel at home in the Bijou. The pillars, the walls, the seats, the lighting, the drapes, the screen, the usher, nothing seemed right. And especially the audience. They were kind of snooty. They weren't her kind of people. At the Royale they were her kind of people. She felt comfortable there.

"Well, I better go and get ready," Laura said. "Albertina will be here any minute now." She went to her room.

Albertina Braga was their next-door neighbor. She was Laura's age and she worked in a sweatshop making dresses. She and Laura always went to the movies together. Well, they had to. Ma wouldn't let Laura go unless she went with Albertina. And Albertina's mother wouldn't let Albertina go unless she went with Laura. One Sunday Albertina was sick and Laura wanted to go to the Royale alone. "No!" Ma exploded. "No, Laura! Only cheap girls go to the movies alone. The boys see you there alone. They think only one thing."

"What do they think?"

"They think you're there to be picked up! You think I don't know these things?"

"And what happens if Albertina moves away or something? Does that mean I can never go to the movies again?"

"No. Then you will go with your brother."

"Him!" Laura was outraged.

"Then you will go with me. Or your father. But you will not go alone."

And that was it. She never did go alone. Of course, Laura had to admit—by now she was so used to going with Albertina, she wouldn't go alone even if Ma said she could. She wouldn't be comfortable sitting all by herself. That was why she and Albertina were so concerned about each other's health—if either one got sick, no movies.

"Ma, will you come in here and tell me what color shoes I should wear with this dress?" Laura called from her room.

Ma went.

"That's a fine thing," Pa said. "What color shoes to wear. Laura lives like a rich girl. She has a closet full of shoes. She will never wear those shoes out. She has enough shoes right now to last her for the rest of her life, even if she walked up and down the streets all day long. In Portugal you had one pair of shoes—if you were lucky. You wore them only on special occasions. If you were going to town, you carried them till you got there so as not to wear them out. And, yes, I knew many who could not afford leather shoes. They wore wooden shoes. Yes. Wooden shoes. Do you believe that? Wooden shoes."

By now Ma had rejoined Pa and Seraphin, and finally Laura came out of her room. She was all dressed up and smelled strongly of perfume. She seemed self-conscious.

"How do I look, Ma?"

"You look fine, girl," Ma said, laughing. "Don't worry."

"I hope Albertina hurries up. I don't want to be late. You're late, you get lousy seats."

The movie began at two o'clock, but the doors were open at one forty-five.

Ma was sitting by the window, watching Albertina's house.

"Oh, Laura, here she comes."

"Okay! Bye, everybody! See you later!"

Laura dashed out.

"Bye, girl. Have a good time. Enjoy yourself," Ma called after her.

The two girls met on Laura's front piazza, and they walked briskly off down the street. Ma watched from the window.

"What time is it? Did you look?" Albertina asked.

"It's a little past one-thirty."

"Then we've got plenty of time."

"Not for good seats," Laura said. "I don't want to sit way in the front. Or way in the back either."

"Did my mother tell your mother about my new job at work? I'm kind of excited about it."

"No, she didn't. What is it?"

"Well, of course it's just a temporary thing, until Sophie comes back. She was hurt in a car accident. Anyway, on Monday I was sitting at my place, sewing, and the boss came up to me and said, 'Albertina, you're a good stitcher, but how would you like to work in Shipping for a while?' I says sure. I was thinking it's better than being a stitcher and if Sophie ever quits, I could maybe get her job."

117

"So what do you do?"

"Well, mostly, I have to keep track of all these boxes of dresses. I have to know where every style is, every size, every color. We have all these shelves going the whole length of the Shipping Room and as the girls finish them I store the boxes of dresses on the shelves, and then I have to take certain boxes down depending on the order to be shipped out."

"Do you like doing it?"

"Yes, a lot. It's challenging to keep track of everything. And also, I'm moving around. I'm not sitting in that one chair for eight hours. But there's just one fly in the ointment. It seems there always has to be one."

"What is it?"

"When I put the boxes of dresses on the top shelf, I have to climb this big ladder. And when I do, the guy in charge of the Shipping Room rushes right over. He wants to hold the ladder for me, he says. But I know he does it just to look up my dress. I'd like to drop a couple of boxes right on his goddamned head."

"Why don't you complain to the boss?"

"Are you kidding? The guy in charge of the Shipping Room is the boss's son. And Daddy is very protective of him. I know I'd be the one to get blamed. And I'd be the one to get fired."

"And another thing he does," Albertina continued, "is there are a couple of places in the Shipping Room where you're cut off from the view of other people, and when I'm in one of those places, he's sure to follow me there, hovering near me. He makes me nervous. I think he's getting his courage up to put his hands where they don't belong."

"What will you do if he does?"

"I think I'll just tell him, 'Look, Norman, don't come around here looking for some cheap feels. You're going to marry some nice Jewish girl someday, so wait till then.'"

"I'm glad I'm not in your spot," Laura said.

"And the funny thing about it is when he's near me, his lips are always wet. He's only twenty-three and his lips are always wet. It's like he's drooling."

"Did you tell your mother?"

"Do you think I'm crazy? Do you remember Manny Amaral's sister on Bullock Street? She was a waitress and a guy propositioned her and she told her mother and her mother went out looking for the guy with a knife. I don't think my mother's that way, thank God, but there's no telling what she'd do."

They waited at the corner to cross the Avenue.

"How'd your week go, Laura?"

"Oh, you know. Shitty. How would you like to be called a crook in front of a whole store full of people? This Polish lady made a scene. She claimed I cheated her on a weighing. She was yelling out, 'You a crook! You a crook!' I felt like saying to her, 'Lady, if I ever steal, it's going to be for dollars. It's not going to be for two cents.'"

"What I don't like about your job is the hours. I only work till noon on Saturday. You do to eight o'clock, don't you?"

"Yes."

Now they were on the same side of the Avenue the Royale was on.

"Say, Laura, before I forget, did you happen to listen to the Theatre of Chills on Wednesday night?"

"Yes, I did."

"Oh, good. Because I was listening and halfway through my father made me stop and go hold some wallpaper for him in the other room and I never did hear the ending. What I wanted to know was this. You remember that guy, Hilary Layton, he went swimming in Dr. Kane's pool and when his fiancée jumped in the pool all she found was Hilary's skeleton. How did Dr. Kane kill him? Did he put some acid in the pool or something? How could he turn him into a skeleton that fast?"

"No, he didn't use acid," Laura said. "It was done this way. Alongside the pool Dr. Kane had a little secret room, a compartment underwater, you know, and this compartment was full of those piranha fish, the kind that eat human flesh. As soon as Hilary dove in the pool, Dr. Kane pressed a button and it released the door to the secret compartment and the piranha all came out and ate Hilary. It just took seconds."

"Yes, but when Hilary's fiancée jumped in, nothing happened to her."

"Yes, but remember she had gone upstairs to get a towel, so she jumped in about five minutes after Hilary. That gave Dr. Kane plenty of time to get the piranha out of the pool."

"How did he do that?"

"He had the piranha trained. He struck a gong three times and the piranha all went back into the secret compartment and he pressed another button, which closed the compartment door. So there was no trace of them in the pool."

"Wow. What a clever murderer, huh?"

"Yes. After I heard that story, I think I'd be scared to get in anybody's swimming pool, wouldn't you?"

"Yes."

The Royale was in the middle of the next block. They could see the theatre marquee sticking way out above the sidewalk.

A young man was approaching them. He was walking toward them, away from the Royale. Laura glanced at him. He was not looking at them. He was looking straight ahead.

Laura made an instant judgment: He was a greenhorn fresh off the boat. You could always tell. It wasn't just the strange cut of his suit coat. It wasn't just his squeaky shoes. It seemed that all shoes made in Portugal squeaked. But even if you put American clothes and shoes on him, you could still tell. It was in his face. There was a wild, untamed look in his eyes. Like he came out of a jungle. There was something in his eyes that was too raw, too pure, too concentrated. America had not had a chance yet to melt him down, to burn that fire out of him. Portuguese boys born in this country did not have that look. And the ones who were born in the old country gradually lost it.

And Laura had noticed another peculiar thing about the greenhorns. They came over and they were always dark. Not black, but copper-colored. A dark red-brown copper color. But that color changed. The longer they were in America, the paler they got. The whiter they got. In fact, look at the Portuguese kids born in this country. Most of them were as white as regular Americans.

As the young man came up to them, to Laura's surprise Albertina greeted him. "Hello, Anibal!" Albertina said in a friendly way.

He did not speak but half-bowed gravely to Albertina. He did not even look at Laura. And he kept on going.

"Who is *that?*" Laura said in kind of a nasty way.

"Oh, that's Anibal. He works at my place, in the Cutting Room. He's a spreader, walks back and forth all day, spreading cloth. He's very nice. He's very, very polite. The girls all tease him but he won't have anything to do with them. He got here a while back from the Azores."

"I would have guessed he was a greenhorn," Laura said.

"Don't laugh at the greenhorns," Albertina said. "They get here, they put the whole family to work, they save every penny, and in two or three years they own a house. They end up with more money than you or me."

"They shouldn't let them in," Laura said. "With all the unemployment, they're taking jobs away from Americans."

"That's true," Albertina said. "The bosses love to hire them."

"Why?"

"Because they'll work harder than you or I will. They'll run, if you tell them. They're so scared."

"They shouldn't let them in," Laura repeated.

"Well, don't forget, your father and my father were greenhorns too and not so long ago," Albertina said.

"That was different then," Laura argued. "Gaw had a lot of jobs then. The mills needed workers."

"But it's hard on their kids," Albertina said. "You remember that Portuguese girl last year in the South End? She walked into the ocean because her father wouldn't let her see this boy. And there's a girl I work with, Philomena. Her father takes her whole pay. He won't give her as much as a thin dime. She can't even go to a show. She's like a slave. And he makes her wipe her bottom with pieces of newspaper. The father's saving money by not buying toilet paper. And then the newspaper plugs up the toilet and the father calls the landlord to come and unplug it. And the landlord gets all mad. He wants to kick them out."

A pustulous usher, dressed like Napoleon, was out on the sidewalk in front of the Royale. "Immediate seating available," he intoned. He would go on saying this even after all the seats were sold.

Laura and Albertina got at the end of a small line. Each bought her own ticket. The sober-faced, middle-aged Frenchman who ran the Royale collected their tickets at the entrance and they hurried inside.

The doors had just opened. They pretty much had their choice of seats. The Royale had three sections, one in the middle, and one on the left, and one of the right. There was no upstairs, like the older Globe had. Laura liked to sit in the right section, about one-third of the way up from the front. She always sat on the aisle seat, with Albertina on her right. That way she was protected from both sides. No repulsive person could sit next to her.

Laura really enjoyed this part, sitting in a lighted theatre, relaxing in her favorite seat, contemplating her good fortune, while all around her people scurried and bustled about and called to each other, in a hectic and frantic search for seats. That was why she always tried to get here early. It was worth it. And by two-fifteen, after the picture had started, all seats would be taken. The Royale was always a sellout on Sunday afternoon.

All week long Laura had looked forward to this moment. Anticipation is perhaps the sweetest pleasure of all and a long afternoon of perfect enjoyment lay ahead. Two good pictures waiting, waiting for the curtain to pull away from the screen, waiting for the dark to settle over the house, waiting for the sudden roar of the sound track, waiting for *the beginning*. Laura loved the movies. When she entered a movie house, all the contentions and hurts of everyday living dropped away from her as if by magic. And all her natural suspicion and skepticism were left on the street outside. She was the perfect audience. She had the capacity, the ability to give herself over completely to the picture. It didn't matter if the picture was good or bad, although she of course preferred a good one. Her acceptance was total. If the director wanted her to cry, she cried. If the director wanted her to laugh, she laughed. If the director wanted her to be scared, she was scared. And of the three, crying came the easiest to her. The slightest hint of a dog dying or, Heaven forbid, a mother dying or a son leaving home or a girl giving up her lover, and the tears flowed copiously.

To be allowed to sit with her, Albertina had to abide by certain unwritten rules. No comments on the picture. No idle chatter. No questions. No talking, period. And absolutely no guessing what was going to happen next. Laura *knew* what was going to happen next. She didn't need anybody telling her. But she didn't want to think about it. She willed herself to live in the picture only to that present moment and not beyond and so whatever happened always came as a surprise to her. And above all, no criticizing the picture. Even if there was a lot to criticize. Because criticizing the picture absolutely destroyed Laura's sense of belief and complete trust and spoiled the whole afternoon for her. Fortunately, Albertina was wonderful. She understood and was the perfect, silent companion.

And then suddenly it happened. The velvet curtain parted and flowed away from the screen, the second transparent curtain began to move, the light vanished, the dark was there, the sound track opened powerfully, and it started. Laura sighed happily. In no time at all, they were in a lawyer's office high up in a New York skyscraper. It was a very well-to-do lawyer's office, with dark wood everywhere, leather chairs, paintings on the wall.

Mr. Pettifoy, the old white-haired lawyer, was very dignified but he still had a twinkle in his eye. He was talking to a girl and you could tell he really liked her. And the girl was obviously rich; you could tell from the way she acted, she was so carefree about everything.

The two of them were talking.

"You mean to say that I came all the way from Paris for nothing?" the girl said.

"Now, Miss Marsden, you know as well as I that I cannot alter the terms of the bequest," Mr. Pettifoy said. "At twelve noon on your twenty-second birthday, in this office, you are to receive one million dollars, providing you have met Stipulation 1A."

"And what is Stipulation 1A?"

"Stipulation 1A says that you must be married and your husband must accompany you to this office."

"Well, of all the—I never heard of such a thing!"

"My dear girl, your late Aunt Agatha felt that the wedded state would help settle you down and moderate your . . . wildness."

"But I don't have a husband!"

"Precisely my point. I could not have stated it better. And your birthday is tomorrow. So it would seem you have lost the bequest.

Unless, of course, you can come up with a husband in the next twenty-four hours."

"How can I possibly do that?"

"I am sure I have no idea. But did you not just return from a year's travel in Europe? I should have thought you would have met some dashing young men somewhere on the Continent."

"Oh, all those counts, kissing my hand. Their mustaches tickled."

"By the way, young lady, your guardian, Lord Harnley, has invited you to a dinner party at his residence this evening. He expects to see you and your husband."

"But I don't have a husband I've told you!"

"Miss Marsden, twelve noon on your twenty-second birthday is—" he looked at his pocket watch "—exactly twenty-three hours, twenty minutes, and thirteen seconds away. I suggest you get to it without a moment's delay."

"Get to what?"

"Get to capturing your Prince Charming," Mr. Pettifoy said with a wicked smile. He held the door open for her. "Good day, Miss Marsden."

She walked out with a puzzled look on her face.

The scene then shifted to the busy streets of New York. The girl was in a limousine. There was a uniformed chauffeur driving. You could see from her expression that the girl was trying to decide what to do. Suddenly they came to a park.

"Bosley, stop here!" the girl commanded.

She got out of the limousine. She was wearing a beautiful mink coat and her hair was done just lovely. Laura wished her hair could look like that.

The camera closed in on the back of a man sitting on a park bench. The man was a bum. His clothes were a mess. Especially his hat. There were three or four pigeons at his feet and he was feeding them peanuts, but he was doing it in a wonderful way. He wasn't feeding them like most people feed them, rather glumly. He had given each pigeon a name and he talked to each one as he threw it a peanut. "This one's for you, Josephine." He was making jokes with them. He was obviously having a good time.

The girl stood on a park pathway, undecided which way to go. Then she spotted the bum. She walked toward him.

"You there!" she called imperiously.

123

The bum gave no sign that he had heard her. He kept on feeding the pigeons and talking to them.

She was angry. She came up to the bench boiling mad. "You there! I've been calling you!"

The bum excused himself to the pigeons, deliberately, without haste. And then he turned to the girl and for the first time you saw his face. It was Cary Grant! Oh, he was so cute! Even needing a shave, he was cute. Cary Grant was Laura's favorite actor. Most girls liked Clark Gable the best, but she didn't. Gable was too much a roughneck for her.

When Cary Grant finally turned to the girl, there was a beautiful smile on his face. "Yes, miss?"

"Didn't you hear me calling you?" she demanded.

"Oh, was that you?" He still had that beautiful, disarming smile on his face.

"I take it you could use a handout," she said crisply.

"A handout?" he said, looking puzzled.

"Yes, a handout," she said impatiently. "You're a bum, aren't you?"

"I'm a vagrant," he corrected her. "No, I don't need a handout, thank you very much. I'm doing quite nicely, as a matter of fact. Maybe tomorrow—if I see you. But today I've eaten," he said, indicating the bag of peanuts. "Would you care for one?"

She shook her head disdainfully.

He cracked the shell and tossed the peanut up in the air and caught it in his mouth.

"Oh, you're impossible," she said. "What kind of a bum are you anyway?"

"A happy one."

"Well, if you don't need any money for today, take something for tomorrow."

"No. If I take something for tomorrow, that means I'm thinking about the next day, and if I start thinking about the next day, then pretty soon I'd start thinking about next week and then next month. I'd start to worry about the future. Then I'd have to get a job. That's why I only take one day at a time. I've found I'm much happier this way."

Then she broached the idea of a temporary job. The job was to pretend he was her husband. They, of course, wouldn't really be married and all that implied. It would be strictly for the benefit of others. Cary

Grant wasn't really keen on the idea but he finally accepted the job. But she didn't tell him why she was doing it—to get the million-dollar bequest. And then they went off to buy him some suitable clothes.

The next scene, after a succession of quick stops at very fancy men's clothing stores, took place at Lord Harnley's dinner party. People were standing all about, talking to each other. The camera panned around the room and then zeroed in on the girl. She was standing alone, and in a close-up of her face you saw that she was very worried. She was watching Cary Grant, who was over to one side. He looked great in evening clothes, tails and all, and, of course, he was clean-shaven. He was talking animatedly to Lord Harnley, who was listening closely to him. Lord Harnley was a bluff, hearty Englishman. He was played by C. Aubrey Smith.

"This is not generally known yet, sir, but there has been a big copper find in the Voska Mountains," Cary Grant was saying. "There is no question that an investment in Bramwell Limited stock at this time should pay big dividends in approximately six months."

"Bramwell stock? H'mmm. And I was going to sell mine."

"No, sir. I would buy, not sell."

"How do you know this?"

"I went to school with the son of the chief geologist for the company, sir, and we keep in touch."

"Capital! Capital!" Lord Harnley slapped his thigh. "All right, Peter, I'll buy!"

Cary Grant just smiled. Peter was his name in the movie.

Lady Harnley then took hold of the girl's arm. "Darling, I'm just dying to meet your Peter."

"Yes, of course," the girl said, but you could see she was reluctant to have Lady Harnley meet him.

But Lady Harnley steered her over to where Cary and Lord Harnley were.

"Winthrop, I want to meet him, too," Lady Harnley said to her husband. "Don't keep him all to yourself."

Lady Harnley had a lovely chain around her neck and from it hung a silver pendant. Cary Grant looked at the pendant with interest. "What marvelous workmanship!" he said. "Made in Spain, wasn't it? I'd say sixteenth century."

Lady Harnley was both pleased and amazed. "Yes, but how did you know?"

"I say, old chap!" Lord Harnley exclaimed. "How would you like to come work for me? I've been looking for someone like you for a long time."

Lady Harnley turned to the girl. "Darling, tell me, where did you two meet? I'm sure it was very romantic!"

"Why . . . why. . . ," the girl stammered.

Cary Grant quickly broke in to rescue her.

"We met at a little get-together the Maharajah of Jodhpur threw on the Riviera."

Lady Harnley's eyes were wide. "You *know* the Maharajah?"

"Oh, yes," Cary said very casually. "I've been with him on several tiger shoots in the jungles of Malaya. Desi—that's what his friends call him—is quite a sportsman."

The girl couldn't help but try to needle him. "How was it in Malaya?" she asked mischievously.

"Hot."

Just then the wine steward came up to Lord Harnley.

"Sir, for the wine this evening, would the Chateau Rothschild 1926 be satisfactory?"

"That sounds all right to me," Lord Harnley said. "What do you think, Peter?"

The girl looked up at Cary Grant, alarmed. You could tell what she was thinking. How could he possibly know anything about fine wines? Would he make a fool of himself now and give the whole game away?

"I find the Chateau Rothschild a bit tart myself," Cary Grant said smoothly. "May I suggest the Chanton Mouton 1921?"

"An excellent choice, sir!" the wine steward said. You could tell he was impressed.

By now the girl was starting to look at Cary in a new light. You could see the admiration in her eyes. She didn't know it yet, but she was falling in love with him.

Oh, it was so funny! If one of the guests mentioned a certain hotel in Italy, Cary had stayed there and knew the old bellhop. If someone mentioned a certain chef in Paris, Cary had eaten his specialty. And a lady at the party had for years searched for someone who knew how to mix a certain drink and Cary got up and mixed it.

Oh, it was a good picture! It was so good! How he tamed her out of her spoiled ways.

They fooled everybody and of course the girl got her million dollars. But then a servant inadvertently let it slip out why the girl had hired Cary to play the part of the husband, and Cary was very hurt. He had thought the girl really liked him and here she had done it only for the money. So he walked out on her. And she was frantic, looking for him, because she really loved him. And then she thought to look in the park. And yes, there he was. At the same park bench she had first seen him. Only now he was not wearing his bum clothes. He was wearing his nice clothes and he was shaved. He was feeding peanuts to the same pigeons. Only now he wasn't enjoying himself. He wasn't talking to the pigeons and making jokes. He was sad.

127

The girl walked up to him, but notice, she had come to the park without the limousine and chauffeur, without the mink coat. She came humbly.

She sat on the bench by his side.

"Could I have a peanut, please?" she asked.

He didn't answer. He just looked very unhappy.

"Please, Peter, won't you come back?"

"What for? You've got your money now. You don't need me."

"Oh, Peter, I don't care about the money, don't you know that? It's you I care about. I've already told Mr. Pettifoy what I've done, that I cheated, that I wasn't really married, and I've given him back the million dollars. So don't you see, you fool, it's you I really want. I love you, Peter."

And she started to cry.

So Cary threw a peanut in the air and she caught it in her mouth. Then they both laughed. And as the picture ended, they were sitting on the park bench kissing and a pigeon was looking up at them quizzically.

The lights came on.

It was Intermission.

"Wasn't it good?" Laura just shone.

"Yes," Albertina said.

Everybody was talking, stirring, getting up, going to the bathroom, going to the lobby to buy popcorn, candy bars, gum.

"I think I'll go back and get something," Albertina said. "Do you want anything, Laura? I'll get it for you."

"Yes!" She was too lazy to get it herself, to stand in a long line back there, but if Albertina would get it, that would be great.

Laura gave Albertina a nickel. "Get me an Old Nick." An Old Nick was the biggest and heaviest candy bar you could get for a nickel, and she believed in getting her money's worth.

Albertina left, and Laura looked around the theatre briefly. Despite the many people who had left their seats, there was still quite a crowd seated. In short, it was the usual Sunday story—the theatre was packed.

Laura took note of who was sitting directly behind her and Albertina. Two young French girls, both about fifteen years old. She had heard them chirping away in French before the picture started. The two girls were in the act of spreading out a white handkerchief on one seat and leaving a brown pocketbook, without any money in it you could be sure, on the other seat. The handkerchief and pocketbook would act as claims on the seats while the girls were back in the lobby.

Laura liked Intermission. Some people didn't, but she did. Intermission was a break in the movies. It gave her a chance to relax. It gave her a chance to enjoy the delights of memory, the memory of wonderful scenes in the first picture. It gave her a chance to anticipate with pleasure the picture yet to come. And now that Albertina had been willing to brave that line, it gave her also a delicious candy bar to think about tasting. And eating a candy bar in the dark was always more fun than eating it in the light when you felt people were watching you and envying your every bite.

Laura leaned way back in her seat and kind of slumped, so that her head rested on the top of the back of her seat. She looked up at the ceiling. She looked up at the Cupid with his bow and arrow painted over the plaster. She looked up at all the little lights. If only life could be as enjoyable as this, she was thinking. If only life could be like sitting down and watching one big long enjoyable movie.

What Laura could not know was that she was about to play a part in her own movie. A phantom silently slipped into the seat behind her, sitting on the spread-out handkerchief. The phantom leaned forward. His lips almost touched Laura's ear. He murmured, *"I kiss your feet, Laurina."*

Aaaaaahhhhh.

The words caught her like a spear through the heart. Consciousness was falling away from her. She was spinning, spinning, spinning through space. She could not breathe. There was a constriction in her chest. Dying must be like this.

She lay back, helpless, passive, impaled on the words. Physically, she could not move. But within she was in turmoil. She felt an excitement, a surging, a beating, a crying she had never felt before in her life.

No voice had ever spoken like that to her before. A voice of passion, humility, love. A voice that carried everything before it. To think that someone felt that way about her—it was beyond imagination. She had never expected this. She had dreamt of a kiss on a park bench, yes. But not this. This was different.

Out of a clear blue sky—bang! And in five seconds her whole life was changed.

She knew who it was, of course. She had known before the second word had passed into her ear. Anibal. She had never heard him speak before, but she knew it was him. Outside the Royale today was not the first time she had seen him. She had thought so at the time. But now it flashed back with sharp clarity. A Sunday morning at Mass. Her attendance at church was poor, but several weeks ago she had been there. A crowded church. She felt something boring into her back and turned and looked unerringly at where the rays were coming from. Two burning eyes. Anibal. She had forgotten it until this moment.

The two French girls returned behind her. She heard them talking. Albertina came back and handed her the candy bar.

"What a mob back there," Albertina complained. "I thought I'd never get my turn. And when I got up to the counter, this guy, this Frenchie, cut right in front of me. The nerve of some people."

The lights went out. The second picture began.

It was frightening, because this was no game. With the Americans dating was fun. First this one, then that one, and so on, ad infinitum. The Americans did not condemn and ostracize a girl who had dates with different fellows. In fact, the opposite. She was prized as a popular girl. But the Portuguese saw that girl as used goods. The Portuguese played under a different set of rules. With the Portuguese your first date was your last. Your first date meant you were spoken for. Your first date was your first step to the altar, a firm first step. Therefore, you had to be fantastically careful who you had your first date with.

In other words, for the Portuguese the picking and choosing came before the dates, not after. By the time the first date came around, the picking and choosing had already been done. That was why how you looked at someone was fraught with risk. If you looked at him the wrong way, he could interpret that as encouragement and assume you were interested in him.

Looks were dangerous. Your eyes could not stray casually. Every look had meaning. A returned look established a claim. One look and you were betrothed. It was nothing to fool with.

Laura was in a panic. The seriousness of the situation terrified her. What should she do? She did not know. How did she feel about Anibal? She did not know. She had to be careful. There was risk. There was danger. There could be no false steps.

Albertina suddenly broke into her thoughts. "Laura, are you all right?" she whispered.

"Yes, why?"

"You look funny. And you're not eating your candy bar."

The candy bar lay in her hand, unopened. She had forgotten about it. She unwrapped the end and thoughtfully took a bite.

Laura had not turned around since it happened. Not in a million years would she have turned around with the lights on. But now, in the safety of the darkness, she did. She took a quick look behind her at the sea of faces. She did not see him. But she knew that somewhere out there two burning eyes were watching her.

For the first time in her life she lost track of what was happening on the screen. Her mind kept wandering. The noise of the picture began to give her a headache.

She felt queer. She felt a rushing tingling like someone had seen her naked. She felt a blinding, tearing excitement that made her want to cry out, to shriek. She felt a doom. She felt a heavy knowledge, sure and final, a sadness beyond consolation. She felt everything and all at once, exhilaration, misery—it was too much. She felt like she was going crazy.

The picture ended.

They went out. There was no sign of him.

The phantom was gone.

They walked along the Avenue.

"That Cary Grant is really something, isn't he?" Albertina said.

"Yes," Laura agreed, without enthusiasm.

They walked in silence for a while.

"What's come over you, Laura?" Albertina asked in exasperation. "Usually I can't get a word in edgewise with you, and today you haven't said two words since we left the show. Are you mad at me? Is it something I did?"

Laura laughed weakly. "No, it's nothing you did. It's just me, Albertina. Don't pay any attention to me."

Just as they were about to turn off the Avenue, a car drove up to the curb and the driver leaned across his passenger and called out the open window, "Laura!"

Hearing her name really startled Laura, but she composed herself and went over to the car.

131

Albertina followed.

It was Max, Benny's younger brother. Max owned and ran a very successful smoke shop in a prime location downtown. He sold cigarettes, cigars, pipes, magazines, things like that. The rumor was that he took in horse bets on the side.

Every now and then Max and his wife came to the fruit store. She was with him now. She was sitting in the front seat next to him. She had a full, ripe figure. She always looked the same—an imposing head, half-lidded eyes, and the beginnings of a secret smile like she knew something you didn't. She was loaded down with jewelry—rings, including a big diamond ring, jangling gold bracelets, dangling earrings, a necklace—and none of it looked like cheap stuff. They must be going to someplace special.

Max was the opposite of Benny. Benny was always sour-faced and grouchy. Max was always friendly, cheerful, expansive.

"How's the election going, Laura?" Max boomed at her.

"The election?" Laura said dumbly.

"Yes. Are you telling all your customers to vote for Benny?"

"Oh, yes, Mr. Shapiro," Laura said. "I tell everybody I think he'd make a great Mayor." She hadn't spoken to a single person about it.

"Well, we appreciate everything you're doing. I know Benny is not the type of man to tell you that, but don't worry, deep down he appreciates it, too."

"I'll do my best," Laura said. "I've even been telling my friend

Albertina here to talk it up for Benny among the girls at her shop."

"Yes, she has," Albertina said.

"That's great!" Max enthused. "Because you know, every vote counts!"

"That's right! One vote could win it!" Albertina agreed.

"Keep 'em flying!" Max said, and he drove off.

The girls continued up Cosgrove Street.

"Do you think Benny will win?" Albertina asked.

"No. I don't think he'll get ten votes. He's a Jew, and nobody likes Jews. Who's going to vote for him?"

"If I was voting, I might."

"Why?"

"Because the Jews are smarter than the rest of us. You remember how they were in school? They were smarter than us."

"That's not necessarily true."

"Well," Albertina said, "if they're not smarter than we are, then answer me this. How come all the Portagees in this city are working for Jews in the sweatshops and stores, including you and me, and how come there's no Jews working for any Portagee?"

Laura was silent.

Albertina was loath to let go of a good point. "How come we're working for them and they're not working for us?" she asked again.

Laura didn't answer.

"That's why I think it might not be such a bad idea to have a Jew for Mayor," Albertina continued. "They're smarter than anybody else, so why not pick out the smartest one to be the leader?"

"Benny's good at figuring numbers but I think that's about all he's good at," Laura said. "He's certainly not very good at meeting people. He's too suspicious. He thinks everybody's trying to cheat him. But I hope to God he wins. Then he wouldn't have so much time to spend spying on us. And breathing down our necks. He's like my shadow. Wherever I go, he goes."

"Do you think Secundo B. Alves has a chance?" Albertina asked. "There's a lot of Portagees in this city."

"I'll tell you the God's truth," Laura said with sudden exasperation. "Pardon my language, but I don't give a shit as to who's running or who wins the election or anything. I wouldn't care if Santa Claus was running."

Albertina was taken aback by Laura's vehemence.

They walked for a while without saying anything, and then Laura said, "Your father and mother are both from the Continent, aren't they, Albertina?"

"Yes."

"So are mine. Do you know anything about the Azores?"

"No. Not much. I know they're a bunch of islands and they're somewhere out in the Atlantic Ocean, that's about it. Why?"

"Oh, I'm just curious. My father said that every island in the Azores is different. He said on one of them, I forgot its name, all that the men do is sit around all day and play sad songs on their guitars and cry after every song. And there's another island, it's off the beaten track and so no ships ever stop there, it's more isolated, you know, and so the people on this island never got civilized. The men are ignorant and brutal and they stick each other with knives. I wonder what island that boy is from who works at your place. What was his name—Anibal?"

"I don't know," Albertina said. "But I can find out for you. I can ask him."

"No, don't do that!" Laura said hastily.

"I would say this," Albertina said. "From what I've seen of him, I think he came from the island where they sing sad songs and not from the island where they knife each other."

133

CHAPTER 12

FINIS

The Primary Election for Mayor of Gaw came in mid-September. Benny lost. Secundo B. Alves lost. Lawyer Grabonski lost. John "Jack" Doyle lost. Armand Langevin won. Mayor Mayhew won. It meant that Armand Langevin and Mayor Mayhew would face each other in the Final Election in the first week of November.

It was strange about the election. The coincidences. Seraphin had never seen Secundo B. Alves before in his life—and then he saw him three times during the election. He saw him the first time making that speech in the Ponta Delgada Social Club before the Primary. He saw him again between the Primary and the Final Election, and then he saw him the third time on the day of the Final Election. And after that, he never saw him again.

The second time he saw Secundo B. Alves was in Cozy Grimeaux's garage. Cozy Grimeaux sold new Studebakers. His place of business was separated into three parts and it started on the corner of Beal Boulevard, across the street from Seraphin's corner. First came the used-car lot, which Cozy shared with a Cities Service gas station. Here Cozy sold his trade-ins. He had about ten of these used cars for sale, and each of them had a message painted in white letters on the glass of the windshield, like "A pippin! Only $125!" Next came a big garage where the cars were fixed. Then came a small showroom with a big window where Cozy had on display a couple of brand-new shiny Studebakers.

Cozy Grimeaux stood out in the North End of Gaw. His hair was always parted and slicked down with some shiny stuff. You never saw one hair out of place on his head. He had pit marks all over his face and a thing growing out of the side of his nose, like a wart. But the main thing you noticed about him was his clothes. He was a very flashy dresser. He had one outfit where he wore a bright yellow sport coat and bright red pants. You sure noticed him in that. And he owned a lot of suits but he dressed mostly in sport clothes. Usually the sport coats were not a straight, solid color. The color might be blue, but it would have different shades of blue in it. Often the coats had stripes in them or squares. The stripes usually went up and down but he had one coat where the wide stripes went sideways and he looked like a convict. And his shoes always looked brand new. They were always highly shined and almost always light brown in color. They made a lot of noise when he walked because he had metal tips on the heels and the soles.

Seraphin liked Cozy Grimeaux because he wasn't one of your crabby store owners. A lot of store owners didn't like kids and they gave you a sour look when you walked by. But Cozy never did. Of course, he never smiled and said hello either. That would have been going too far. Actually, Cozy looked like a guy who had a lot on his mind. He looked like a guy who was worried. And he was very nervous, rarely standing still. He was always talking a-mile-a-minute to somebody and at the same time edging away from that person. It always looked like he was trying to get away from whomever he was talking to.

Cozy Grimeaux got interested in politics this election, and naturally since he was French, he backed Armand Langevin. When Langevin got by the Primary and became a finalist, that really spurred Cozy on in his efforts. One Friday night he had a big rally for Langevin in his garage. All the cars had been moved out, the place cleaned up, and folding chairs brought in and set up row after row. Free gifts and movies were promised, so Seraphin was, of course, there. And Cozy got a pretty good crowd, even after you subtracted the kids. Well, it was free, that was why.

The free gift turned out to be a balloon, which really didn't thrill Seraphin too much. What can you do with a balloon except blow it up? So he kept his in his pocket, unblown up. He would save it and then maybe he could trade it with somebody for something else. Almost all of his things he had gotten by trading.

The movie turned out to be about ten minutes long, and it was a real dumb movie. It showed these girls; each one would turn and smile prettily at the camera, and then she would climb this ladder and dive off into a pool. The girls were modeling all the different styles of bathing suits that were on the market. The movie announcer kept making what he thought were funny remarks and he never shut up. Yes, it was true that the girls were very pretty and had nice figures and they were good divers, but it was still a dumb, boring movie. There was no plot, no excitement, no action. Besides, the swimming season was over for the year. But what can you expect when it's free.

After the movie came the speakers. One after another, telling the audience what a great guy Armand Langevin was and why you should vote for him. After an hour of this, Seraphin was ready to go. But somebody passed the rumor, which later proved to be untrue, that there would be another movie in a little while, so Seraphin stayed on, stoically half-listening to the speakers. A quartet of French girls came out and sang a song to the melody of "My Blue Heaven" but the words were all about how Armand Langevin was going to be elected Mayor.

And suddenly Seraphin sat up straight. For the Master of Ceremonies, a big fat guy, said, "Tonight we have a surprise guest—one of the outstanding political leaders in this community—Mr. Secundo B. Alves! Let's give a big hand to Secundo B. Alves!"

And Secundo B. Alves walked out on the stage, waving to all the people, with a broad grin on his face, and walked right up to the microphone.

"First of all, ladies and gentlemen, I want to thank all the voters who supported my candidacy in the recent Primary. I look upon every vote cast in my name as a sacred trust. And that is why I stand before you tonight.

"I must confess that I had not meant to do any more public speaking in regard to this election after the results of the Primary became known to me. I meant to keep silent. However, many of my friends counseled otherwise. They continually pressed me to make my personal judgment known to all. 'You have a duty to speak out, Secundo,' they said to me. 'This is no ordinary election,' they said. 'The city is at a crossroads.'

"I did some soul-searching and I decided that I had no right to be silent in a perilous time like this. I must break my silence. I must speak out. My conscience will not allow me to do otherwise.

"My friends, a momentous decision is before the citizens of this city. What kind of a city do we want? Do we want the city of Mayor Mayhew? What do we have? We have high taxes. We have waste. We

137

have unemployment. We have stagnation. Is that what we want? We need to attract new industries to Gaw. What is Mayor Mayhew doing about this? Nothing! Nothing! And more nothing! How many years is Mayor Mayhew going to have to serve before we turn him out?

"One man can set this right, and that man is Armand Langevin. I will tell you all, right here and now, that Secundo B. Alves stands foursquare behind the candidacy of Armand Langevin for Mayor! I have known and respected Armand Langevin for many years. A man with sound business sense, a man who is a proven success in his chosen field of endeavor, he has always worked for the public good in this great city of ours.

"The Portuguese people of the North End know they have a true friend in Armand Langevin. And I want you to know, my friends, that I shall be spreading that message among all the Portuguese people of this city! The Portuguese people want Armand Langevin to be Mayor of Gaw. They need him. But it is not only the Portuguese people who need him. The French people need him. The Polish people need him. The English people need him. And all the other nationalities need him. We all need him. In him the various nationalities of this city see the ideals, the dreams, and the goals we all hold in common. He will unify all the diverse nationalities of this city as no one has ever done before, and together we shall all march to victory!

"Oh, my friends, I cannot tell you how good it feels to be here tonight to support the candidacy of this wonderful man. I am proud to add my voice to the growing army of Armand Langevin supporters. Armand Langevin is a man you can count on, a man you can trust. Let us go forward and get the job done. Let us give the people of Gaw a new deal. We can win this election. Yes, that's what I said. We can win it. We can win with Langevin. Win with Langevin!

"Oh, ladies and gentlemen, I have a vision. I see a vast and pitiless ocean to cross. And I see one ship, leaking badly and guided by an incompetent, timid landlubber—Mayor Mayhew. And I see another ship, the good ship *Spirit of Gaw*, commanded by Captain Langevin. And I see the *Spirit of Gaw* plowing bravely through the unknown sea, a sea full of peril and danger. And in the dark of night comes a violent storm. The sea is running wild. The waves are mountainous. The wind is shrieking. The proud mast sways before the fury of the wind. The ship groans in the ferocity of the storm's attack. And on the storm-drenched deck I see Captain Langevin at the helm. His grasp is firm. And when so many on the voyage have lost hope, I hear his calm voice—'Do not despair, my friends. I shall take you to a safe harbor.'

"And he shall, if we give him the chance. And we must give him the chance. Thank you, ladies and gentlemen."

There was tremendous applause and whistling and stamping the feet. In fact, Secundo B. Alves had gotten the biggest hand of the night.

Seraphin applauded, but he was really shocked. Somehow he had never thought that Secundo B. Alves would give a speech for Armand Langevin. It just didn't seem . . . right. He had thought that Secundo B. Alves had been serious when he spoke in the Ponta Delgada Social Club, but this made it seem more like a game.

139

After that rally in Cozy Grimeaux's garage, there wasn't much going on about the election. October passed. The election was winding down to its final day.

Then the day before the election, the weather changed drastically. It got bitterly cold, like it does in January and February. It seemed to clear a lot of people right off the streets, but one person it didn't was old Fred Farnsworth. Seraphin was walking along the Avenue when he noticed Fred standing in front of the Bullock Street fire station.

Fred was wearing his old green overcoat. It was the strangest shade of green you ever saw. It was a pale musty green. The coat looked liked it was at least fifty years old. It had a mothy, chewed-up black velvet collar.

Fred had a woolen scarf wrapped around his head, like the old women wore, to protect his ears. His hands were red and cracked. His nose was dripping. He kept knocking his shoes together to keep his feet warm. Or alternately hopping up and down for the same reason. He was cold all right. In fact, he was freezing.

Fred wasn't walking anywhere. He was standing in one spot, handing out the small election cards for Armand Langevin to any passers-by who chanced to come along. And there weren't many.

Seraphin was a little disturbed to see Fred doing this. Usually bums did this kind of work and Fred was not a bum. He was poor but he was not a bum. Bums drank and stuff like that. Of course, Seraphin knew that Fred wasn't doing this because he liked Langevin. This was a job. He was getting paid for it. Pa had explained that to him, why people stood around on the Avenue and passed cards out. But he didn't think that Pa knew that Fred was doing this. At least Pa hadn't told Seraphin he was, and Pa would certainly have mentioned it.

Seraphin didn't know what to do. Fred never talked to him first. He was too shy. Should he talk to Fred first? Or would it embarrass Fred too much? Knowing that he had been observed doing bum's work? Should Seraphin just pretend that he didn't see him and just look across the street as he walked by him? No, they were the only two people on the street. He couldn't help but see him. To heck with it, Seraphin decided. He would talk to him.

"Hello, Fred," Seraphin said.

"Hello, Seraphin," Fred said. He managed an embarrassed smile.

"It's mighty cold today, isn't it?" Seraphin said.

"Aye, aye. That it is."

Seraphin loved the way Fred said aye for yes. He had thought only sailors said it, "Aye, aye, sir." But Fred had told him that everybody said it in the part of England he was from.

"Would you like a card, Seraphin?" Fred asked him gravely, showing him Armand Langevin's wavy hair and jutting jaw.

"Yes, I would."

Fred had some difficulty separating one card from the mass with his numb fingers, but he finally made it. He handed the card to Seraphin.

"Thank you," Seraphin said.

"I'm not supposed to give any to you young people, but I don't think anybody will mind too much," Fred said with a slight smile. He began knocking his feet together.

"Well, I've got to be going," Seraphin said. "So long, Fred."

"Good-bye. Good-bye, Seraphin," Fred said, smiling and nodding in a friendly way.

And Seraphin walked on.

The next day came, Election Day. It remained bitterly cold. That night Seraphin was coming home after spending two hours at the North End Guild, which was only open in the evening from seven till nine o'clock. The Guild was like a boys' club. The kids had fun there. The Guild had a basketball court, a pool room with four pool tables, another room with two Ping-Pong tables, and a game room where you could play checkers, tiddlywinks, and sit-down games like that. The Guild was in an old house on Sharples Street but it wasn't a tenement house. The rooms in it were so big it had to have been a mansion at one time. It cost twenty cents a month to join the Guild.

So it was that Seraphin was walking home along Beal Boulevard on Election Night a little after nine o'clock. He came to Cupp Street, one block away from his street. He saw a car coming down Cupp Street so he didn't try to cross the street but stayed on the corner.

The car coming down Cupp Street was a shiny brand-new Studebaker. It came to the corner where Cupp Street crossed Beal Boulevard. Normally drivers stopped here, looked both ways, and then went across Beal Boulevard. This car stopped at the corner with the motor running but didn't go across the Boulevard. There was no traffic so they weren't holding anybody up, but it seemed kind of funny to stop in the middle of a street.

141

Then the back door of the car opened. Gee, it sounded like they were having a party inside the car. A man was singing a song with the confidence and the enunciation of a drunk. And his words played against girlish shrieks of laughter. The wisecracks by the girls were coming thick and fast; they were all having a good time.

Then a light went on inside the car, and Seraphin saw who was singing. It was Cozy Grimeaux, dressed in a very expensive-looking camel-hair topcoat. Cozy was in the front behind the wheel. Beside him was a girl a lot younger than he was. She was in her twenties. Her hair was done up very elaborately, like she had just stepped out of a beauty parlor. She had bright lipstick on and plenty of rouge on her cheeks. And her clothes were very nice. She definitely looked like she was going to a party or had just come from one.

In the back seat was another girl. She was a twin to the girl in the front seat in every respect but the face. And there was a man in the back seat. He stepped out of the car and made his way to the gutter just a few feet from where Seraphin was standing. He bent over and started throwing up into the gutter. It was Secundo B. Alves.

While they waited for him to empty his stomach or for his stomach to empty itself, Secundo B. Alves's companions did not quiet down. The wisecracks, the singing, the laughter kept right on. Only now one of the girls was singing and Cozy was cracking the jokes.

Then Secundo B. Alves made his way back to the car and fell into the back seat. The girl reached across him and slammed the door shut.

The light inside the car went out. And the car accelerated with such suddenness that the tires squealed. The car shot across Beal Boulevard and Seraphin didn't move. He watched the car until it went out of sight.

Somehow, he really wasn't surprised. Somehow, he sort of had been expecting something like this to happen. Although it was a strange piece of luck or coincidence that he should be the one to witness it. Yet maybe he was the one who was supposed to witness it. He had seen Secundo B. Alves at the Ponta Delgada Social Club. He had seen him at the rally for Langevin. Maybe that was why he had been chosen to see him this third time.

He continued on his way.

He felt a great and sharp sadness. Was this how everything turned out? In defeat? In disappointment? In unhappiness? He assumed that Langevin had lost. There was something unhappy about that car. They weren't celebrating anything. They were drinking out of desperation. He felt that just as if they had put a sign on the car.

When Seraphin got to his street, he turned the corner. There just a few feet ahead of him was Fred Farnsworth. Fred didn't see him. He had just come out of the small grocery store on the corner and was on his way home. Fred lived in a low-ceilinged attic tenement four houses past Seraphin's house.

Seraphin did not catch up to him. He didn't want to. He didn't feel like talking to anybody. Fred was carrying a small bag of coal on his shoulder. That's how you could tell who was really poor. Wait for the wintertime and then watch. The people who had enough money, like Pa, had a ton or two of coal delivered into the coal bin in their cellar. But the people who were poor had just enough money to buy a small bag at a time.

Fred tried to stay out of his freezing tenement during the day. He went to the library. And he spent two or three hours every afternoon in the tenement of Mrs. Bumpus, a widow who lived downstairs in Seraphin's house. Mrs. Bumpus was really old, in her seventies, and she never left her tenement any more. But she had lots of coal. She burned a lot more than Seraphin's family did. Fred visited her every afternoon and the first thing he did was shovel the ashes out of her stove into a pail and then he took the pail outside and dumped it into an ash can. Then Fred took her two pails, big ones they were, down cellar and filled them with coal and brought them upstairs and set them by her stove. Then, if she needed anything, he went to the store for her. And he always told her the news because her eyesight was not good enough to read a newspaper. And they talked. They sat close to her stove, which she kept red-hot, hotter than Seraphin's family kept theirs. And after a while Mrs. Bumpus always said, "How about a spot of tay, Fred?" That was how she pronounced tea.

"Oh, don't fuss now," Fred would say.

"Oh, it's no bother, Fred. No bother. And how about some toast and marmalade to go with it?"

"Well," Fred would say slowly, like the perfect guest, "that would be very nice. Very nice indeed."

143

And sitting by the warm stove, sipping the hot tea, munching on the toast, and puffing on his pipe afterwards, that was the happy time of the day for Fred. You could tell it from his voice. That was the happy time of the day for Mrs. Bumpus, too. You could tell it from her voice.

And that was how Fred stayed warm in the afternoon. But now it was nighttime and he had to stay in his own freezing tenement.

Seraphin looked at the tall, thin figure in the green overcoat ahead of him, carrying the small bag of coal on his shoulder, and he started thinking. How was it decided who had the ton of coal in his cellar and who the small bag of coal on his shoulder? Who decided that? There didn't seem to be anything wrong with Fred, yet he ended up with the bag on the shoulder. Why? People were sorted out into those who had enough and those who didn't have enough. How was this done? And when he got older, would he be one of those who didn't have enough? Would he end up with the bag on the shoulder? That was a frightening thought.

When he got home, Ma was listening to the returns on the radio.

"Mayor Mayhew is winning," she told him. "By a landslide. By several thousand votes. That Langevin doesn't have a chance."

Seraphin nodded.

"Your father will be happy with this," Ma said.

"Yes," Seraphin agreed.

That was just about it, he thought., The election of 1934 was over.